DEAD-NOT-DEAD

JAY ISHINO

DEAD-NOT-DEAD

JAY ISHINO

For B.D.R.
You really were a spectacular asshole.

CONTENT WARNING

This book features scenes involving graphic violence, blood and gore, attempted suicide, character death (on page), sexual assault, and attempted rape.

THE SOUNDS of footsteps startled my eyes open. I hadn't been dozing, more like lying around staring at my eyelids.

I skittered up and chucked my Bowie knife. A pair of boots dodged my shitty throw. It wasn't until I looked up that my brain registered it hadn't been a dead-not.

Brandon picked up my knife, which hadn't even come close to hitting him. "Not gonna kill anything that way, Nats."

"Well, this bullshit just started. You can't expect me to be an expert already." I dusted off my pants. "How does one throw a knife that results in death?"

"Depends on lots of things: weight and length of knife, distance to target."

"With this knife," I said, grabbing my knife from him and sheathing it, "I'd have to be close then, eh?"

Brandon moved closer to me. "Fifteen feet with a

lunge, easy. Throwing with that lead arm maybe even twenty, whilst still hitting center mass or even face."

So far, I'd used my Bowie knife for close combat, stabbing dead-nots between the eyes and whatnot. No one had ever given me a throwing lesson, and I felt the need to scribble this in my notebook. When I reached for it, Brandon put his hand over mine.

"I can show you. You don't know something like that until you do it. Tactile learning."

He didn't pull his hand away, and I kinda didn't want him to. Heat spread through my body. He looked at me so seriously then, but didn't do anything except move his hand to my hip and remove the Bowie knife.

"Okay," I breathed.

He wrapped his hand around the handle. "Overhand throw, so it only does a half rotation."

When he threw the knife as he'd said, it behaved the way he'd explained before sticking into a tree. I had to snap my mouth shut before I started drooling all over myself. This was supposed to be a lesson, not an excuse to get all hot and bothered.

I swallowed the lump in my throat as he retrieved the knife and passed it back to me. "Thanks."

"Try it. Give you more of an idea of what I'm saying."

So I did. I puffed up my chest, thinking it couldn't be *that* hard, and threw the knife like he'd explained. It didn't go as planned.

My first throw grazed the side of a tree, falling flat into a tangle of nearby roots. He corrected my grip and posture for the second throw, and while it still didn't stick into the tree, it flew a little better toward my intended target.

I tried not to let my feelings overwhelm me, but I couldn't help thinking that I needed Brandon. Would there ever be anyone who knew so many things about literally everything and could help me through this world? It was hard for me to believe that someone like Brandon even existed, let alone that it was possible he'd chosen to stay here with me.

He helped me almost daily to survive and gotten me out of more than one situation that could have resulted in me being dead or even dead-not-dead. I wanted him near me always, yet I couldn't shake the feeling that being this close to Brandon would not be in my best interest.

I wish it had been easier to count the passage of time since the end. The simplest technology like clocks taken for granted. It'd never been important until we lost everything. Now I had a pressing need to know just how much time Brandon had spent in my life so I could see how much I'd stand to lose without him there.

"I have a question," I said, sheathing my knife again.

"Maybe I have answers," he said.

"Can we do this again tomorrow?"

"Duh." Brandon hovered close to me for a moment before pressing a kiss to the top of my head.

"Same time?" I asked.

He nodded.

ONE
NOW

CREATURES SUCH AS FLEAS, ticks, and tapeworms, to name a few, get their delicious nutrients by robbing the host of theirs. They're nasty, awful parasites, and the world would be a helluva lot better without 'em. Unfortunately, the shitty world we're stuck with is full of parasites. Dead but not dead, walking parasites.

Brandon, who always had a cigarette between his lips, exhaled a heavy waft of smoke which hung for a second in the crisp morning air before it vanished.

"Those'll kill ya," I said.

"Can't die," he said.

He was right, I suppose. We survived. It's what we did.

Using the metal ladder leaning unsteadily against the side of the house, I'd climbed up to the roof. A sea of brick-red, tiled roofs, belonging to suburban houses, spanned as far as I could see, not one more distinguishable from the rest.

More interesting than that, though, was the view of Brandon. Brandon was skinny, unbelievably skinny for someone his height. Unless he was wearing a hat, his greasy jet black hair, which was never styled, usually hung in front of his eyes like it did now.

His scruffy face, with just the right amount of black stubble, looked good instead of mangy. He might've groomed himself this way, but I knew he didn't. Not much point making that effort in this day and age.

With his pants hung so low around his hips, they should've fallen off any second. But for as long as I'd known him, he belted them tight that way.

Practically oozing cool like his prized collection of t-shirts, Brandon was also ridiculously smart. He could talk for hours about space, chemistry, and physics, but also easily talk about books, comics, and movies. Anyone who looked at Brandon, an emaciated hoodie-wearing, tattooed freak, wouldn't think he'd be as smart as he was. But looks can be deceiving, and when this guy spouted out everything from Stephen Hawking to Greek mythology, he baffled the hell out of everyone.

Not one for traditional mornings, he'd been up here since the middle of the night and would probably sleep during the day. I yawned, rubbed my eyes, and surveyed the area.

The yard of this particular house was surrounded by a nine-foot cinderblock wall in the back and a chain-link fence around the front of the property, which made it somewhat safe. Safer than others, anyway.

Close to the fence lay a pile of dead-not-dead ones, stragglers who'd made it too close to our encampment. Brandon must've taken them out sometime during the night.

After our brief greeting, he didn't say much else to me, super-focused on the task at hand, night watch, and on smoking.

I pulled my hoodie together, zipping it up, and flipped the hood over my head. The sun wasn't doing much in the way of warmth today. I watched the ash he tapped down from his cigarette flutter like gray moths, disappearing into the roof tiles.

He rubbed the almost-spent cigarette out on one of the brown-red tiles and picked up an airgun. Because these were non-lethal, I stared at him, confused as to his intentions.

A few dead-nots were scattered around, snarling, drooling, and looking all nasty. Some walked barefoot, with shredded clothes. But mostly they stood around unless triggered by something, like motion or sound.

They could also smell us, especially when we'd sweat. Once they got a whiff, it was like a beacon as they dragged themselves in our direction.

It was easy to spot the newly turned dead-nots from the older ones. Like people, they came in all shapes and sizes from grotesquely malnourished to obese, and everything in between. But the newer ones were a lot less gray with some color left in their cheeks.

No matter their body type, each one walked around looking like they'd been sprayed with blood at some point because well, they undoubtedly had. It was both fascinating and disgusting at the same time, kinda like a car accident. No one wanted to look, but sometimes we couldn't help it.

Raising the airgun, Brandon took aim at a dead-not some sixty yards away. The thing, swaying like a tree in a gentle breeze, had its back turned on another one who stood close to it.

"Brandon—"

"Natalie . . . Nats . . . Nat . . . shh . . . ," he said in a lilting, singsong whisper.

Brandon fired a pellet, and it hit the one who had its back turned. It spun with a snarl and swung its arm toward the one behind it a couple times until its nails sank into the tender flesh of the other. The victim of the prank lashed out, and the two tumbled over. They wrestled around on the ground for a while.

Giggling, Brandon set down the gun, and lit another cigarette.

"What are you like eight years old?" I asked, narrowing my eyebrows.

"Affirmative," he said matter-of-factly.

Shifting on my feet, I wanted to talk to him, not about anything in particular; I just wanted to be around him. But it was clear from his terse answers he wasn't in the mood.

The past crept into the silence between us.

I met Brandon long before what the media called "The Collapse" happened. With no formal education, Brandon was a machinist, making him a very handy person to have around.

He hated cops and stories with happy endings, but he loved Parker Posey and whiskey. He also loved PB&Js and tomato soup eaten together as a meal. Gross, right?

With no rhyme or reason, he had tattoos everywhere—his leg, back, an unfinished sleeve. The tattoo spiraling around his left wrist was a nod to one of our shared favorite movies. Though he'd gotten it before I met him, I was still giddy to meet someone who had a great love for that film too.

Hardly ever wearing a shirt at home, he drank the shittiest cheapest beer either in his house or in a dingy dive bar he considered a second home.

Whenever we'd hang out, he would take some hits off his bong, and we'd fuck and then lay in bed and watch TV or talk about books, comics, or movies, or anything really.

Sometimes the mental stimulation was more powerful than the physical. I loved listening to him talk about everything he stored in that massive brain of his.

Other times he'd play music illegally loaded onto his computer or show me videos. He wanted me to love all the things he loved, but I not only loved everything he introduced me to, but tragically, for me, I also began to love him as well.

Did I want to fall in love with Brandon? I wish I

could say "no", but then that would be a lie. Did I want to be his girlfriend? Every day. Every day for five years I did.

I wanted to run my fingers over his skinny body hoping to absorb everything he knew about science, pop culture, obscure anime, about the world. I wanted to bathe in his knowledge and to drink up everything he gave me like a starving vampire taking its first victim in ages. I wanted all he had to give and more.

Unfortunately, he never loved me. I know that now. To him I must have just been a place to put his dick, someone to relieve his boredom.

Jokingly, Brandon and I used to talk about our zombie apocalypse plan. We agreed we'd find each other. We'd raid my father's gun storage and the train tracks, as there are apparently a lot of weapons there, and include the stockpile of pointy objects in Brandon's house.

We'd fight. Every day we'd fight. We'd do it together.

My need for him became like a drug addiction. I could get clean of Brandon. Sometimes I could stay away from Brandon. But I would forever crave him, and I would always try to claw my way back to him. There were times I'd relapse into his arms, a song and dance we did for the five years we spent together.

But time tends to separate people like it separated us. Though he wounded me many times in those five years, one time almost ended me. After that, we stopped talking, or to be more specific he stopped talking to me, and we finally went our separate ways.

In the interim, the time I spent without Brandon, I found pieces of him in everyone I met but more so in those I formed relationships with, romantic or otherwise. They were people who resembled Brandon in some way shape or form, but they were never really all of him.

Brandon, in his entirety, was unlike anyone I had ever met. Irreplaceable. I was most attracted to people who reminded me of Brandon somehow. People who liked the unusual kinds of books he liked, people I could watch cool TV shows with, people I could have intelligent and meaningful conversations about random subjects with. But no matter how hard I tried, I couldn't substitute him with another person.

When shit hit the fan, I went to find Brandon. Why? For one, I had little hope that I could survive the end of the world on my own, and Brandon by my side increased my chances of not dying by 150%. And two, I knew he'd still be alive. He was smart, wily.

I found him right where I left him, obviously alive, high as a kite, and covered in blood. In one hand, he held a katana, his prized possession and a gift from his half-Japanese friend's aunt. He never could remember where she lived in Japan.

In his other hand, he gripped a can of warm beer, in a beer cozy no less. In the middle of his driveway, he rocked a patio chair off its two front legs. With blood sprayed all over it, the concrete beneath his feet looked like some grotesque Jackson Pollock painting.

We hadn't seen each other in a while, maybe two years or so. Even though I looked a little different, he recognized me. Five years with someone doesn't mean forgetting about them forever when it's over. That's the kind of person Brandon was. If ever somebody fit into his world, he'd remember them forever.

His eyes were red and glazed over. His roommates and their dog were nowhere to be seen.

"Nat." He pushed himself up in what looked like slow motion, and when he finally got to his feet, an eerie stillness overcame him.

"Let's go," I said, grabbing his arm.

He didn't move forward, instead staggered back.

"Get in the fucking car, Brandon." I tried to make my voice firm, but it didn't matter because he had no choice.

He clearly had nowhere else to go, with no one else; I couldn't see another soul anywhere. Eventually, he loaded up a backpack, mumbling about not being *that* attached to his any of his gear.

When he finally got into the car, I didn't ask him where everyone else was or why he'd been covered in blood. A simple change of clothes hid the need to talk about anything as fucked up as what had actually happened to the world.

That was maybe one or two years ago.

When we met others, other survivors like us, I pushed hard to join them. If nothing else, I knew that with other people around, I could suppress that longing deep in my gut easier than I could when it was just the two of us riding around trying to survive this shitty world on our own. I didn't want to feel like this forever when deep down I knew he'd never want me the way I wanted him.

Now on the roof with Brandon, watching him fire on those dead-nots made me feel so fucking nostalgic that I had to try super hard to ignore the urge to reach out and grab him.

Because the roof was angled, the whole time I'd been dancing around, constantly repositioning my feet. When that wave of nostalgia hit me though, I inched a little closer to him. My foot got caught in one of the tiles, and I pitched forward.

Of course, my dumb body had decided not to fall backward toward the safety of the cinder-block guarded backyard. Nope. I continued to tip forward where there was a compromised chain-link fence and a mountain of dead-nots waiting to catch my fall.

But I didn't plop onto a bed of dead-nots. Brandon grabbed my arm, and I could see he'd dug his combat boots into two broken tiles.

He pulled me up and flipped me onto the other side of the roof. His eyes bore into mine, which were watery with the tears I refused to let fall.

My heart threatened to beat out of my chest, and I couldn't say whether it was from what had just happened or the way Brandon looked at me, like something important had almost been ripped from him. I understood that feeling because I felt the same way.

"Careful Nats," Brandon said.

"Yeah." Shaking, I crawled toward the ladder, and

before I climbed down, I looked back and said, "Thank you."

He didn't say anything, only nodded at me as if to say "no problem."

Later, safely in the house, I decided to make a to-do list. From my back pocket, I pulled out the small unicorn notebook I carried and scribbled in it.

To-Do List:

1. Survive

2. Get Brandon back

It struck me then, one of these things would be infinitely more difficult than the other.

TWO

INSIDE THE HOUSE, the remaining members of our group, five of them anyway, were mulling around doing different tasks, trying to get us set up for the week. Surveying the busyness of the interior, I noticed there was one person missing.

In my search for Chloe, I felt like I kept getting in someone's way wherever I went. Since I didn't see her in the main part of the house with the kitchen or great room, I figured she'd probably be in one of the five bedrooms.

I quickly found her in the first bedroom I checked. She leaned toward the sink in the large open bathroom and scrutinized her appearance, her face almost close enough to touch the mirror.

"Look at all this sun damage," she whined.

Hovering in the doorway, I looked over Chloe. A former model, she had the trademark body: legs that didn't seem to end, long jet-black hair, and full pouty lips. Because she'd been a lingerie model in the real world, she also had these perfect, large silicone breasts. Bless.

Dragging my eyes away from her, I looked down at my body. By comparison, I was short, the shortest one among us, made even more comically small because I always seemed to be surrounded by tall people. I never liked my average sized breasts—read small—but somewhere along the way I decided I didn't mind my wide hips and thick quads.

Feeling super self-conscious, I stuck my hand in my mousy brown hair, cut just past my shoulders, and tried to comb out some tangles with my fingers.

Chloe had been busy this morning, rummaging through the drawers looking for makeup, probably trying to maintain some normalcy in this shitty world. She'd scattered various eye shadows, lipsticks, and blushes and now looked over a virtual rainbow of color in front of her. Without looking, she tossed me some foundation she'd found. I caught it before it hit the floor.

"Ugh, only house we find with make-up, but it doesn't match my skin color!"

You'd think the world wasn't being overrun with dead-nots, as lack of proper makeup was her biggest problem today. I looked at the foundation in my hands. Chloe was right, though; it was way too light for her golden-brown skin.

I never knew why she cared so much about maintaining her appearance. Maybe she hoped things would go back to normal one day and her looks would become a money-maker once again.

Chloe said her Indian mother had married a Japanese man, and as she told it, she'd ended up with her father's hair and her mother's skin. Second generation American, her mom had initially disagreed with Chloe's life choices before The Collapse. Chloe's mom ended up being unbelievably proud of Chloe when she made it big as a model and had always been her biggest fan.

I sometimes envied Chloe's life before The Collapse. Not because I wanted to be a model. I assuredly did not, but because she had money and fame and supportive parents. Living the dream.

Looking like she didn't want to be bothered by the makeup setback, she settled on some brightly colored eyeshadow and black liner, both of which she applied expertly around her eyes. Like a little bird in a cage, she twittered at me while she put it on.

I couldn't even focus on what she was saying. This was a common pattern of behavior for Chloe and me. Her world before had been nothing like mine, and I often found it difficult to relate to her.

Before I could say anything, she pulled me out of the doorway and inside the bathroom, slamming the door behind me. I heard the click of the lock.

"Chloe?" A voice that I immediately recognized as Carson's tried to push through the door.

"I'm doing my makeup! Not a chance in hell Carson!" Chloe shouted back.

Hard to believe Carson had never seen Chloe without make-up. My skin prickled with excitement. When she pulled me into the room with her, I didn't even care what she looked like, because I knew she had plans for me.

"That's fine. I'm letting everyone know Brandon and I are making a food run. We'll be back before dark. Stay in the house," Carson said.

"Yes, sir!" Chloe saluted him from behind the closed door.

Carson's response, a loud scoff, resounded from the other side of the door.

"Don't poke an eye . . . ," he said, the words fading away.

In every endeavor, there needs to be some form of leadership. I think we're built that way as a society, flocking to those who are natural leaders.

For a few years now, Carson held us all together, kept us moving, and made sure we were always safe. Before the dead-nots, I imagine people either loved Carson, or they hated him. I'm sure even those who hated him couldn't doubt his natural leadership ability and probably respected him for that.

Even though he had gray hair, he never looked like an old guy. Maybe he was somewhere in his forties? We never got that information out of him, but then again, no one really talked much about age these days. Another thing that just didn't matter.

So Carson remained the biggest mystery of all of us because whenever he spoke, he focused on talk of survival: making food runs, securing weapons or ammunition, or planning where we were headed next. He certainly didn't have time to discuss the

weather, nor was he interested in any kinds of pleasantries.

Watching Chloe with makeup in the bathroom mirror was pretty cool. I was never any good with makeup. She tried to make me over many times before, but like an angry cat, I always fought her off. I didn't see the point of it in this world. Try telling that to a former model.

As I sat on the counter and ogled her now, I noticed something I hadn't before. Chloe didn't have shoes on, a stark contrast to the combat boots I almost always wore. Also, she had on the tiniest shorts that could still be called shorts and a tank top that revealed more cleavage than I'd ever seen in my life. It struck me as odd because none of us ever seemed to get so comfortable. We were always on guard.

In addition to proving ourselves with an edge weapon, Carson had a couple of caveats for joining his group. In the beginning, if Brandon and I hadn't agreed, we'd have been out on our asses. These were Carson's Core Values, and as he explained, what kept him, and all of us, alive.

First, he told us that no one would ever be left behind for any reason.

"We don't leave people behind. We're a group, a team, and we do this together," he'd said. "If someone is injured or sick, even if they're bitten, it doesn't matter. No one gets left behind."

Second, everyone was to adhere to the buddy system, strictly adhere.

"If anyone has to, for whatever reason, leave

camp, number one, you must first discuss it with the group. If they allow it, number two, your buddy must accompany you. If not, forget it."

At the time, I wrote Carson's words in my notebook:

Asshole Carson's Core Values:

1. Don't leave anyone behind.

2. Stick to the buddy system.

Chloe always wanted me as her buddy. She refused to be with anyone else. I have no idea why she liked me so much. I'd roll my eyes when she started one of her "When I was a model . . . " stories. I'd roll my eyes right in front of her. I know she saw it because I never made a point of hiding it.

But she always chose me. I couldn't help but wonder why. My great character flaw, I could never figure out why people liked me.

I can't recall when our "game" started. Of course, it was just all play to her because, aside from survival, there was very little Chloe took seriously.

I never understood her preferences, whether it was only me and Carson, or all women and men. I never asked, and she never volunteered that information.

Trying not to question her judgment, I wondered why she was interested in me because most of the time, even I wasn't interested in me.

Even though I'd just felt my whole body flood with heat over Brandon, these days I was all about Chloe. Call me a hypocrite, okay, but I know exactly who I am. I really hate labels. I don't discriminate, and I like who I like. I'm attracted to who I'm attracted to. Gender never really factored into that equation.

In truth though, there were very few people who didn't drool over Chloe. Besides, whenever I was with Chloe, I didn't think much about Brandon.

Among other things, Chloe liked to kiss. So when she locked me in a room with her, I forgot that hell on Earth literally walked around outside our four walls. I also conveniently forgot that she and I had nothing in common.

I know I said earlier that I found myself attracted to people who were like Brandon. Maybe she was, a little.

I'd seen her stab dead-nots in the face time and again, and I'd be lying if I said watching her kick their asses wasn't super hot.

Like Brandon had done this morning, she'd probably turned dead-nots on each other during watches, too. I couldn't say because she always wanted to do her watches with Carson. I assumed so they could make out and have uncomfortable roof sex. But hey, I wasn't jealous.

Soon after that, Chloe and I abandoned the bathroom and her scattered makeup. It didn't take long till we were naked on the floor of the bedroom. We bundled up in a huge blanket she'd found buried in the back of a closet. She nuzzled closer to me, and I couldn't stop kissing her.

Time passed, but I couldn't say how long it'd been. An hour? Maybe two?

All I knew is that Carson and Brandon would be back soon, and one of two things would happen. One: Carson would coax Chloe out of the bedroom, encouraging her to join one of his "family dinners." Or two: Carson would leave her locked in here all night. I'd hoped for the latter.

"You think there'll be a family dinner tonight?" I asked Chloe.

"Oh, I don't know," she said, examining her nails.

"Do you think they're strange?"

Chloe looked like she was thinking for a moment before she said, "I don't mind them so much. Franklin is an amazing chef, and he always makes the yummiest things."

"But the moniker? 'Family dinners.' It's weird, right?" I wondered out loud. "We're not a family."

"So serious, Natalie," she said, moving her lips to my neck. "Family and home are important to Carson. Why do you think we're always camped out in houses?"

Scenes of the dinners flashed in my head. Us laughing. Franklin loudly telling a story, his hands like someone conducting an orchestra. Carson passing around a steaming bowl of something that smelled awesome. Maybe the dinners were Carson's crutch.

Aside from Chloe, nobody really knew much about him. He was always tight-lipped about his time in the real world.

The longer I thought about it, the more I realized the dinners weren't so bad. When we talked and laughed, it helped us forget about the shitstorm outside.

Before I could respond, a loud banging on the door resounded through the room.

"Chloe!"

"Go away, Carson!"

"Chloe, are you alone?" Carson asked.

"No," she looked at me and smirked, and my heart fluttered a little bit. "My buddy hunted me down after you left, so I let her in."

I couldn't help it. I twined my fingers into hers and pressed my lips to her collarbone.

Chloe lied to Carson all the time. She probably lied to me all the time, too. Like that festering dead-not plague outside, no one was immune to Chloe's lies, but it didn't matter. I told myself I didn't care about her enough to let those lies bother me.

Our relationship was all physical, so I figured it'd be short-lived. I spun this around my head this as many times as I needed to convince myself it was true. Still, I don't think Carson knew about us.

Chloe and me were simply on the buddy system and girl friends not girlfriends. Not that we were ever actually girlfriends.

What the fuck was wrong with me? Was I doomed to live out my twenties not ever being able to define a relationship properly?

"Natalie, are you armed?" Carson asked. "Nat?"

"I'm loaded up Carson," I shouted back in between kissing Chloe's lips and running my fingers through her long silky hair all the while praying he'd leave us alone.

"Well, I'll check on you in the morning. Take care," he said.

Then nothing else came from behind the door. Unbelievable. Chloe wrapped her legs around mine, and I shivered with excitement.

Maybe tonight nothing would come scratching on our window. Maybe tonight it would just be us.

But yeah, Chloe's also fucking Carson. One time I woke up in the middle of the night, always been a poor sleeper, and there were some faint impressions on the bed where her body had been, the heat of her long gone.

Clearly, I can't spear her like Carson can. I can't spear anyone without proper equipment, which obviously isn't a top priority in a dead-not plagued world.

I know Chloe and Carson bonded over having similar familial circumstances. Carson was born first generation Mexican, which was the only piece of personal information I knew about him because he'd shared it with Chloe. She figured it wasn't a secret, so she'd told me. She understood him and related to him on a deeper level, more than I ever could.

Squeezing my eyes shut, I tried to forget about every bad thing that had ever happened in my life, but there were too many bad things. And I couldn't forget. When I opened my eyes, Chloe was staring at me, her naturally long black eyelashes casting small shadows on her face.

After one particularly good night with Chloe, I

had to convince myself that I didn't love her. That she was vapid, shallow, self-absorbed. I also tried to convince myself I was an emotional hard-ass, and this world had made me cold. Not loving her was easy. Not loving someone else was unbelievably difficult.

I could never *not* see how beautiful Chloe was though. Forgetting everything I'd been thinking about, I devoured her lips again. I wanted to touch every inch of her, but I also wanted to drag out this moment. To stay locked in this embrace with her for as long as it would take me to forget that the world wasn't shit. Not too long after that, I ended up falling asleep.

When I woke up, it seemed even darker, and ice rippled down my spine. I opened my eyes to nothing staring back at me this time.

"Fuck, not again," I said, digging my knuckles into my eyes.

"What is it?" Chloe's sweet voice echoed from the bathroom.

She stood in front of the mirror, makeup brush in hand. I propped up on my elbow, so I could marvel at her subtle yet precise sweeps.

"I'm cold. Come back," I said.

I couldn't believe how easily she obliged. She slid back down into the blanket, her skin icy. I moved closer to her, hoping to generate some warmth.

"This place isn't so bad," Chloe said.

"Yeah," I said.

I could lie too.

THREE

THE FOLLOWING MORNING, I dressed in baggy jeans and my hoodie. A rich, long-forgotten-yet-familiar smell dragged me out to the back of the house. Brandon and Carson sat on patio chairs around a massive fire they'd built in the backyard firepit.

This house was deep in the gut of one of those cookie-cutter subdivisions. With everything we had here, it looked like we'd be in for a couple weeks of luxury.

"Is that coffee?" I slid into one of the chairs.

"Yup," Brandon answered, extending a cup.

I waved it away and zipped up my hoodie, flipping the hood over my head. I never could stand the taste of coffee, just loved to smell it.

"Found it buried in the cupboard. It's cheap and tastes like shit. However, this house is nicely stocked. Including what we brought back yesterday, we might be able to stay longer than two weeks," Carson said, two hands wrapped around his cup, steam wafting into his nose.

"Nice. But is that a good idea?" I asked, raising an eyebrow.

"I don't see why not. Weather's been rough, and it's only going to get colder. Everyone is tired, and if we can stay safe here for a while, it would be the wisest course of action."

"I could use a break." Brandon wasn't drinking coffee either, and his eyes seemed lost in the flames.

"We all could," Carson said.

I dragged my chair closer to the heat, trying to warm myself up. The morning chill was biting, stinging my exposed cheeks.

"Chloe up?" Carson asked.

"Yep, she's making love to the mirror," I said with a too-real tinge of disgust.

"What else is new?" Carson scoffed. "I'll go check on her."

I dug my heels into the dirt and dead grass as Carson walked back into the house. I decided this would be a good time to clean my Bowie knife, and I pulled a rag I'd found in one of the closets from my pocket.

I was lucky enough to find this Bowie knife buried under some trash in the basement of one of the houses Brandon and I tore up one day looking for supplies. It had obviously belonged to a collector.

Before I got my hands on it, this knife had never seen the light of day. Aside from the case covered in a layer of dust, the knife inside and black handle were in pristine condition, without a single knick on the blade.

Perfect. I almost didn't want to use it. Almost. I kept it sheathed on my belt at all times. All times except when driving, because next to me, it's much easier to unsheathe quickly rather than trying to fumble with it on my belt. I even slept with the thing.

"Oh, my god!" Franklin's voice yanked me out of my own thoughts.

Franklin existed to be a morning person. Even though I hated Franklin, and almost everyone else in the morning, I loved him every other moment of the day. I secured the shining knife and pulled the strings on my hoodie, trying to drown out his chipper sounds inside the fabric.

"Coffee!" He almost squealed, taking the cup Brandon had previously offered me. "Is there anything else? Fake sugar maybe?"

"Negative," said Brandon.

"There's probably not even real sugar." My quiet, annoyed voice emerged through the small opening I'd left in the hood. "I really miss sugar."

Letting out a heavy dramatic sigh, Franklin sipped his coffee and started making adorable little noises of joy as he walked back inside.

Franklin and his partner Jordan came as a set. A cute, but completely opposite gay couple, they were a walking yin and yang. Proud of his Irish ancestry and shock of red hair, Franklin had a particularly optimistic outlook on life and a flair and zeal that was unmatched by anyone I'd ever met. He loved all things bright, colorful, and beautiful. In the face of sudden death, it was somewhat refreshing.

Before the dead-nots, he loved designer coffee, gardening, and lying outside in his cozy backyard, which was teeming with roses. He always had a fondness for roses, he told me once, and when he and Jordan bought their first house, Franklin demanded roses. Thus, his lush rose garden seemed to be continually in bloom. He also loved hugs and puppies.

Franklin changed careers many times throughout his life; he'd been a chef, an interior designer, and right before this happened, a hair stylist, who'd fortunately saved all of his scissors. It was a fucking dead-not apocalypse, and he had shears for cutting hair in a tool belt. No joke. So he always kept us all looking our best without access to a full salon. No one ever said anything about the fact that he sometimes used these same scissors to stab the occasional dead-not right between the eyes.

Once in a while, we'd have to stop Franklin from trying to decorate camp. He doesn't do it so much anymore, but when we first hit the road, he always wanted to add little homey touches like a DIY'd tablecloth or freshly picked wildflowers in places we stayed. Though any roses he came across, he always kept for himself. The problem was, no place was ever home long enough, and no place would ever feel like home again.

Franklin's partner Jordan, a Black man, was completely different from him in looks as well as personality. An introvert, he mostly kept to himself, and when he wasn't stabbing dead-nots right in the brain, spent very little time with anyone besides Franklin. Seeing Jordan somewhere around camp, he would undoubtedly have a history book in his hands and be curled up under a blanket sipping tea.

Jordan hardly ever talked to any of us, so no one besides Franklin knew very much about him. I would come to learn, much, much later, that he really loved hugs too.

I think Franklin became one of my favorite people because we both had a shared love of cooking. I helped him in the kitchen whenever I could and found it equal parts amusing and frustrating to try to make things with only the limited ingredients we could find.

Because Franklin had been a chef, he was better at being creative with ingredients than I was. He taught me so much about cooking that my unicorn notebook was full of things I learned from him.

Franklin's Minimalist Cooking Tips:

1. Substitutions are your best friend.

2. Salty and acidic flavorings belong in everything!

3. Imagination is the key to all the best dishes.

After I felt significantly warm, I went inside to find Franklin in the kitchen.

He had a variety of ingredients spread across the counter and was jotting notes on a notepad.

In the most cheerful voice, he said, "Natalie, my little prep chef, get in here! Oh, I'm so glad I could get you away from Brandon for five seconds."

"What?" I couldn't keep the annoyance out of my voice.

He gave me a knowing look. "Don't play coy with me. You are literally obsess—"

"Wow," I said, cutting him off and gesturing to the food in front of him. "This reminds me of the first year following The Collapse."

He nodded, a serious look falling over his face.

After the death toll climbed well into the hundred millions, the looting cooled, especially in the more populous areas where there are plenty of stores of all types. These days, we still sometimes found things on shelves. The gourmet stores were the first ones picked over. Funny that a dead-not-dead apocalypse wasn't gonna prevent people from eating all fancy. After much trial and error, we learned that abandoned houses, especially those with basements, proved to be better for bringing food back to camp.

In between Franklin's quick and easy cooking tips, we talked about how we ended up cooking side by side, which all started with a dude named Marcus.

"I'd never really been interested in the news or politics or shit like that, you know. I preferred escapes from reality like books or movies rather than spending my time watching the awful state of the world as it continued to deteriorate."

He groaned. "I get it, Nat, but it's important to stay up to date on the state of the world. Or it was anyway."

"I know, but, like, how did anything on the news ever apply to me?"

A scowl fell across Franklin's face. "As an adult over voting age, literally everything that happens in the world should have applied to you."

"Okay, fair point. I know when all this happened though, I was glued to the TV like I assumed the rest of the world was too," I said.

"Right," Franklin said, and then in his best newscaster voice, "Patient Zero has been identified as Marcus Aurelius Kingsmith-Johnson, and no, I'm not kidding about that."

I laughed. "What a fucking ridiculous name, right? I can't help but think the media added 'Aurelius' and like dug through some family records or something for the 'Kingsmith' part. Hell, maybe they made that up."

"Comparing the two, Marcus Aurelius Kingsmith-Johnson sounds so much better blasted out of the TV than Marcus Johnson of Walla Walla, Washington," Franklin said.

I can't remember what they said this clown was doing when he was exposed to a deadly and previously unidentified virus deep in the tropical rainforests of South America. The foul and disgusting virus ate away at him from the inside, withering him down to the bone, and his body came back home in a box.

Had Marcus stayed dead, the rest of the world probably would've never known his name. But when he reanimated on the autopsy table, I imagined the pathologist being scared shitless. After the commotion, several people ran into the room to assist, of course, none of them armed. Boy, did we learn a lot from that experience. Most important being never leave the house unarmed.

Marcus bit four people before dragging his emaciated body out of the coroner's office, a piece of skin from the first incision dragging along the ground. Those four people went out with their friends or home to their families, telling stories of the freak who'd bitten them and how they'd be getting worker's comp. So fucking stupid.

I don't need to explain how virus transmission works. Four people infected six people who infected about six million. And Marcus's plague spread like wildfire.

The government's response started with mild regulations and mandates, but that soon elevated to martial law and later rations. However, the world erupted into chaos until no one controlled anything anymore, and people were scared. I never thought I'd live through an apocalypse. Not recommended.

Because of the lack of government control, riots and looting started. So people often thought other people were their biggest enemy. Maybe they were right.

Now it'd been too many years since we had any system of power in place. Lost track of time long ago. Keeping time didn't really matter all that much anymore in this world; surviving became more important. I mean, number one on my list.

"Do you think Marcus Aurelius Kingsmith-Johnson is still alive?" Franklin asked, stirring a magical smelling stew over the fire. "I remember many scientists publicly claiming they could cure this plague if they could only get their hands on him."

"I don't know, you know. Who knows where he is or what that guy even looks like now? Can he really still be alive *and* have some magic cure inside him?" I frowned.

I couldn't help but think of the resources scientists initially burned through trying to cure this thing and how much better off we'd be if we still had a tenth of that stuff. Thanks for leaving us medical supplies. Fucking idiots.

FOUR

OUTSIDE FRANKLIN CHATTERED AWAY at Brandon and me. I occasionally replied with grunts and other noises. Brandon replied with silence, lighting a cigarette and smoking until his face disappeared behind a cloud.

Little by little, the tension grew, and I hoped Franklin sensed it.

"Okay, darlings! I'm going to plate up this breakfast," he said, slipping on oven mitts and lifting the stew from the fire.

"Need help?" I hoped he could read the pleading in my eyes.

He winked at me. "Oh no, no, no, you helped enough."

And Franklin disappeared inside.

Left alone with Brandon, I remembered my list:

1. *Survive*

2. *Get Brandon back*

I tried to psyche myself up. *Okay, Nat, you can do this. Just talk to him about things he likes.*

On the roof yesterday, Brandon's meager supplies consisted of the airgun, an actual rifle, a flashlight, salt & vinegar chips, and a book.

"What were you reading yesterday?" I asked, trying to make my voice sound like I was discussing the weather.

"Sci-fi." He puffed out more smoke, which became wisps in the chilly air.

This was going well. Fuck. I felt so stupid and awkward, and I chewed on the pull string of my hoodie. Everyone who'd ever spent any time with Brandon, but most especially girls, said that it was like walking on eggshells around him.

"Are you pissed at me?" I asked, apparently about to break a ton of eggshells.

"Negative."

"I hope I can remain in your good graces, then," I said, thinking about when he stopped talking to me before all this happened.

"Hence the communications," he said, the cigarette dangling from his mouth as he fished in the backpack at his feet. "Just don't be dumb."

I couldn't say exactly what he meant by not being dumb, but I assumed it meant that I should neither fall in love with him like before nor do anything to annoy him like before, both of which would prove difficult. "I don't plan on being dumb."

The thick book he now extended to me had a sun-faded blue cover curled at the edges, *The Reality Dysfunction*.

"This is a big fucking book," I said.

"One of three. True, true space opera . . . *every* genre of literature, including porn, included," Brandon said in a very Brandon way.

"I've never read this before."

"You should," he said.

I flipped through the first couple pages. "Thanks."

Brandon didn't say anything else, just puffed on his cigarette.

———

In the backyard, a big oak tree climbed into the sky. I'd been out here every afternoon during the lull of day when no one really had anything to do.

After making breakfast, yesterday's food run hadn't really been sustainable, so Brandon and Carson had gone out again, leaving Chloe and me alone. The distant sounds of dead-nots added an eerie melody to our peaceful afternoon.

For a while, I practiced throwing my Bowie knife.

"Yes!" Chloe said. "That's your best hit today."

With a grunt, I pulled the knife from where it was wedged into the tree just above my head. "That definitely would've been a dead-not head, yeah?"

"No doubt." Chloe motioned at me to come sit next to her in the overgrown grass along the wall.

Never having much desire to say no to her, I

plopped down and pushed my body close to hers, resting my head on her shoulder.

She dragged her fingers through my hair, and I breathed out a soft sigh.

"Can we just stay here? I'm a big fan of this house," I said.

"It's one of the nicer ones, no doubt," Chloe said.

I noticed she'd chosen this spot because it was the most heavily shaded place in the yard. The heat of the afternoon sun didn't touch us here. This moment was perfect.

We stayed like this just sitting close and talking until sunset when Carson and Brandon returned. I didn't want this feeling to end, but I also didn't want to watch Chloe fawn all over Carson. So I got up and went to see if I could help Franklin with tonight's family dinner.

Later that night, Chloe's body curled around mine, and as she slept, I felt her soft breath on my neck. I gripped a flashlight in one hand and the book Brandon had given me in the other. I should've been asleep, but this book was so weirdly interesting that I couldn't put it down.

With a breathy sigh, Chloe shifted and rolled away from me. I pushed the flashlight into the blanket and listened. Her breathing continued in the same rhythmic manner, and I went back to reading.

After about a hundred pages, it became impossible to keep my eyes open, and I passed out on top of the book.

When next I awoke, the room stood shrouded in

darkness, and I heard Chloe cussing. She gripped her toe, and I saw that my flashlight had rolled over to the other side of the room.

"Hey," I said, blinking several times.

"Oh, hi," she said, pulling on a pair of denim cutoffs.

Well, this was a first. I knew Chloe had often left me in the middle of the night for dick, but I'd never caught her in the act before.

"I'm going to walk around the house, having trouble sleeping," she said.

Never in the time I'd known her had she ever struggled with sleep. I pulled myself up into a sitting position. I decided I had two choices here. I could either let her go and try to go back to sleep, or I could start some shit.

"Going to fuck Carson?" I asked, choosing the second choice.

She giggled, which sounded more nerves than anything else. "What . . . Natalie . . . what?"

"I think we should break up." My heart twisted saying these words because it was something I wanted and yet didn't want at the same time.

"Natalie, what? No, I need you as my buddy." Chloe said, brushing out her long silky hair.

"Yeah? Well, I *don't need* to continually lose out to Carson." Okay, that was some serious jealousy coming out in the form of word vomit.

"You're one to talk," she said.

"What? What the fuck is that supposed to mean?" I bristled.

She didn't elaborate. "Carson's really quite sweet, Nat. You don't know him like I do."

"Maybe he should be your buddy then, like fucking permanently." Behind my lips, my teeth clamped together tight, and I rose to pick up the flashlight.

She moved closer to me. "Natalie, what is this attitude?"

I opened and closed my mouth several times, trying to find the words that expressed how I felt. I cared about Chloe and enjoyed what she and I had. But in my head it sounded like *sex good but no love you.*

Chloe tried to take ahold of my hand, the one not holding the flashlight, but I yanked it away from her. I felt bile climb up my throat. I leaned into the air, feeling like I was being pulled downward. Confusion assaulted me from all sides. I thought that breaking up with Chloe would be easier. Fuck. Had I actually caught feelings? No. No. *No.* That had *not* been the plan here.

"Natalie, I really care about you. You're very special to me," Chloe said, and she sounded sincere.

"Nah, all you care about is getting dick." The words felt sharp coming out, but I thought that maybe if she hated me, then this whole break up would be easier.

It was a real Brandon move, I'll admit. Be a huge asshole to the person who'd do anything for them enough times and eventually they'd get fed up and fuck off.

Then anger bubbled up in me, and I wanted to

break something. I tried to throw the flashlight and shatter the mirror, but Chloe caught my arm, and applied pressure, causing me to drop it.

Tears burned behind my eyes as I thought of Brandon. I was never his number one and hadn't been Chloe's either. This time I decided to remove myself from the running for Chloe's number one spot and make Brandon finally see me as his number one instead.

"I think we should break up," I said again, my voice shaky.

The sound coming from my lips was alien to me. I didn't want to lose Chloe, but her inability to choose between Carson and me made the battle for Brandon look like a much easier one.

Chloe looked at me, and I swore I saw a hint of sadness behind her eyes. I wanted to reach out to her, pull her close to me, and run my fingers through her shimmering hair, but instead I pulled my mouth into a straight line.

She took a step toward me, and I shook my head. Then she spun on her heel and, with the soft click of the door, left me alone.

I collapsed onto the blanket, pulling it to my face to stifle the sobs that came on like torrential rain.

FIVE

IN THE MORNING, I felt hungover looking at my red-rimmed eyes in the bathroom mirror. I almost tried to turn on the tap so I could wash my face, forgetting there hadn't been running water in like forever, before walking back into the bedroom.

Sunlight burned through the window, and I grabbed the blanket and wrapped it around me like a burrito. Really could've went for a burrito.

When I finally dragged myself out of the bedroom, I noticed the house was pretty quiet. I breezed by the living room where an oak bookshelf, much too heavy to lift back up, had fallen. I figured out of all of us Jordan had already been rummaging around under the overturned furniture since Brandon was too particular to pick up random books.

In the same room as the bookshelf sat a couch. I almost didn't notice Kelsey, who had curled herself into a ball close to the armrest. I saw her half-brother Omar first, kneeling on the floor in front of her stroking her hair. Feeling like I'd stumbled onto a private moment, I tried to look inconspicuous by staring at the bookshelf. These two were the newest members of our group.

During one family dinner, Kelsey wasn't feeling well and didn't show up to the meal, so Omar told us why she avoided most people at all costs, and it still breaks my heart to think about it. Kelsey and her now deceased husband married young and wanted to start a family early, so they did. They had three children, all nine months apart. This was the American dream for them. Family first. Family always.

"On the worst day of the outbreak, people were still being told it was safe," Omar said. "I remember the news saying '*Maintain a normal life.*' So Everyone went to work. Kelsey's husband went to work. Kelsey, she was a stay-at-home mom, she got the children ready for school just like every other weekday. They were in grades three, four, and five."

Omar swallowed, and the rest of us sat in silence. It was a while before he spoke again.

"The media insisted it was safe. '*This outbreak is under government control. People need not worry. Maintain normal functions,*' they said. So as she always did, Kelsey saw her children to the bus stop. They didn't even make it to lunch. Jefferson Elementary School was overrun with dead-nots in a matter of hours. No child left school that day. I've never been a parent, but I think all parents want to believe school is the safest place for their kids. Unfortunately, that's not always the case."

Before the dead-nots, I'm sure Kelsey was happy and animated and beautiful. These days her eyes, ringed with dark circles, always looked empty. She seemed so frail.

So Omar babied her. When she wouldn't eat, which happened more often than not, he'd feed her. Prone to outbursts, she often shouted out that she wished she was "dead like them."

Whenever I looked at Kelsey, I breathed a sigh of relief that I never brought children into this world or the previous one.

She tried to kill herself before. More than once, really. Omar always caught her before she could do anything to seriously hurt herself.

My heart ached for Kelsey. Truly. But I couldn't help her. No one could, but more than that, there was nothing anyone could do to bring back her children.

When I peered around the bookshelf, I saw Omar whispering to her, and the awkward feeling grew, like I definitely didn't belong there. He turned and saw me. I nodded at him and decided to move to another part of the house, leaving the fallen bookshelf behind.

I envied Jordan who'd probably gotten some uninterrupted book browsing time. I walked around a metal gate that separated the living room and the main hall.

With nothing else to do and everyone seemingly busy, I ended up in a small room that faced the street. Using a pair of binoculars I'd grabbed from the kitchen, I peeked through the blinds.

To the left, I couldn't see anything interesting. To

the right, I spied what I thought to be a dead-not dad. Covered in sprays of blood and pieces of leather that resembled skin, a man with a baby strapped to his chest was sidling through dead-nots, trying to blend in. Whatever he'd done, it worked. They ignored him.

"Carson!" I moved through the house whisper-yelling. "Carson!"

I assumed he'd be with Chloe, yet I still had no idea where to find him. Starting with the primary bedroom, I ran from room to room searching. Fuck this big house. It turned out Carson was back outside by the firepit with Brandon.

"Carson," I said, panting. "Carson, there's someone coming this way!"

"Jesus! Are you sure?" Carson said.

Carson checked his 9mm, and without a word Brandon grabbed his katana and followed me as I led them to the room where I'd spotted the sidler.

The three of us peered through the blinds, dead silent. The stranger had moved closer to our camp.

I think we were more enthralled than anything else. With no concept of time, I had no idea how long it'd been since we'd seen another person. It could have been well over a year. Sad to say, survivors were getting harder and harder to come by. We never knew if most people had died off or if they kept a low profile like we did.

As he came closer to our house, I could see that despite the cold, he was sweating profusely and oddly not wearing any shoes. He looked down at the ground for a moment as if plotting his next steps, but without warning, he turned sharply, stepped back and then his foot went down on a soda can.

The crunch that sounded seemed to wake the entire neighborhood of dead-nots, and they snarled, moving toward him. Two dead-nots became five, and then he was surrounded.

"We need to leave this," Brandon insisted in a harsh whisper.

"He looks like he needs some help. Or at least some shoes." Anything to get my head off the breakup and my stupid to-do list.

Brandon turned to me sharply. "Not our responsibility, Nat."

"Carson?" I asked, trying to force someone else to make a decision, as I didn't do decisions well.

Carson hadn't been listening to our argument. He had now had a firm grip on the handle of his 9mm, which was still holstered.

"If we make our presence known here, we'll have to break camp, and we're not safe anymore," Brandon said through gritted teeth.

"Shut up!" Carson shocked us both into silence with the acidic tone of his voice, and Brandon and I exchanged "what the fuck" looks until Carson finally spat out, "Stay here."

We didn't. We followed him, watching his movements.

Carson walked out of the room and through the house. He opened the front door, not making a sound, and then closed it behind him with the same level of care.

We couldn't look away as Carson walked past the fence and into the street. He twisted a suppressor to his gun and then pointed it right at the stranger.

I sucked in a short, sharp breath. The man saw Carson and moved toward him away from the hoard of dead-nots behind him. He put his hands up and waved his arms frantically.

Brandon moved to open the door, and since neither of us were listening to Carson, I followed Brandon into the yard just inside the fence.

"Thank god!" The man was louder than he needed to be.

"Shut up." Carson spoke in a grating whisper.

Some more nearby dead-nots staggered toward the commotion, joining the one-man party this dude had created.

Since we all carried at least one firearm as well as a blade, I pulled out my handgun and picked off a few that had come the closest. Meanwhile, Carson moved closer to the man, still trying to get him to stop talking.

Unsheathing his katana, Brandon went to work on some nearby dead-nots that had dragged themselves close to the stranger.

After holstering my gun and pulling out my Bowie knife for close combat, I approached Carson to see if I could level with either of them and get all of us back into the house.

But I was too late. Carson had decided he wasn't having any more of this guy's yelling and rousing dead-nots, and got right up into his face, grabbed the collar of his bloody jacket and pulled him roughly toward the house, whispering to him. The man stumbled forward and almost fell onto the baby.

My eyes went wide as I watched the whole thing unfold, unable to move to do anything helpful. Sure, Carson was tough, but I'd never seen him be so forceful like this. The way he treated this stranger seemed excessively harsh, and he'd almost hurt both him and the baby.

Dead-nots were now shuffling from all directions. Brandon and I still had our edge weapons out.

Sometimes the dead-nots are easy to take out. Other times they summon tremendous strength, and I have no idea where a bag of bones would get that from. Probably from the need to feed.

Now behind him, Carson pushed the stranger forward with one hand and, using his other hand, shoved a dead-not away from him. It went flying into another one that was dragging itself toward us, and that second dead-not was impaled on a short pole in the yard across from us. Carson jumped back a step and drove his blade deep into the other dead-not's forehead, leaving the fallen one writhing on the pole.

Too focused on Carson, I'd lost sight of Brandon and my eyes darted around the houses, trying to find him. I spotted him, surrounded by three of them. Without stopping to take a breath, I bolted straight for Brandon. I felt a twinge of regret for leaving the stranger with Czar Carson, but Brandon and I had a history, and I didn't want to see him dead or dead-not-dead.

I took out one of the three dead-nots that had surrounded Brandon by digging my Bowie knife into its neck. When I righted myself, it looked like he was having trouble fighting off the other two dead-nots. He grabbed a hold of one and shoved his camp knife up through its chin and right into its head. Delivering a swift kick to its chest, he watched it fall back. But immediately after that the other one latched its gray fingers around Brandon's arm and started chomping its teeth, preparing to bite him.

With Brandon close to being zombified, adrenaline surged through my body. Maybe I'd been driven by some kind of eternal loyalty toward a man who'd opened my eyes to a world I'd never known before. A world without him in it looked even worse than one overrun by dead-nots.

I jumped on that fucker's back, and I tried to slam my Bowie knife into its skull, but Brandon had already beaten me to the punch by stabbing into the dead-not's neck. When he did, it knocked me off balance, causing my knife to slip and cut into Brandon's arm. The three of us tumbled to the ground. He let out a hoarse cry and shoved all the deadweight off of him, including me.

Leaving me lying on the ground, Brandon got up and stomped toward the house.

So I yelled after him sarcastically. "Thanks for trying, Nat!"

SIX

AFTER ALL OF us were inside the chainlink fence, instead of going in the front door, we ran to the back gate to throw off the dead-nots. Brandon gripped his arm, mumbling his annoyance. Carson continued to push the stranger toward the back door. Feeling chagrined, my eyes remained on my feet most of the time.

Once inside, Carson started barking orders, and emerging from one of the rooms, Jordan almost slammed into the bleeding Brandon.

"What happened to him?" Jordan pointed to Brandon, trying to speak casually, but his voice was tinged with fear. "Was he bitten?"

"No." Narrowing his eyes, Brandon managed, "just cut by a fucking interloper."

"Hey, I almost saved your life," I said, but there would be no gratitude for me this time.

"Come on, let's patch you up," Jordan said.

"Yeah, and take me to the alcohol," Brandon said, no doubt meaning the drinking variety.

The aforementioned "alcohol" meant the half empty booze bottles we kept on hand to use as disinfectants for wounds. Rubbing alcohol had been harder and harder to come by. No matter where we went, though, it seemed like we almost always found at least one bottle or sometimes more of liquor. Full or not, we added it to our stash.

I knew he'd talk Jordan into turning a blind eye while he drank some. Always a silver-tongued devil, Brandon was quite good at getting anything he wanted out of almost anyone.

And then Carson and I were alone with the stranger.

"We should tie this guy up," Carson said.

"What? Why?" I asked.

The stranger didn't say anything.

"Here!" Omar appeared from around the corner and pointed to a metal gate that separated the living room and the main hall.

"Why does he need to be tied up?" I asked, this time trying to assert myself and wondering why this man wasn't arguing about being held captive by people he didn't know.

Carson didn't even acknowledge me and started barking orders. Was I fucking invisible? He told Omar to find something to tie the man up with, and Omar disappeared in the direction of the garage. Franklin came out to see what all the commotion was about.

Noticing him, Carson said, "Franklin, check his pockets. See if he's armed."

Carson grabbed onto the stranger as Franklin patted him down for weapons. His search turned up nothing. Being unarmed struck me as even weirder than anything else. How was he still alive? Franklin produced a wallet with a pretty useless twenty-dollar bill in it and a folded piece of paper.

Franklin passed the paper to Carson, and a puzzled look fell across his face as he opened it.

"What is this?" Carson asked the stranger.

"A map." The stranger's voice was calm, despite his predicament.

"A map to what?" I asked.

"Mecca," the stranger said, and his voice was dreamlike.

Record scratch. Mecca right? What a fucking trope.

The first time I ever heard someone mention mecca, it sparked a bit of hope. They called it "Summer Camp." The name dripped with not only promise, but also a bit of nostalgic joy. Who didn't love going to Summer Camp, right? Because there *had* to be some perfect place, someplace untouched by dead-nots. But the longer we were at this, the more imaginary mecca became, and no one believed in a place like Summer Camp anymore.

So the dream of mecca died a long time ago. Over the years we'd been to many places, and never experienced perfection. I'd never seen a place unsullied or even free of dead-nots.

I watched Carson crumple the map and shove it into his pocket. We knew there was no mecca, but it seemed a bit rough, even for Carson. I thought about how he had walked up to this guy, this stranger, leaving the house without a buddy. Carson was totally off-book today.

Omar returned with some rope, and Carson used his camp knife to cut off pieces to secure the stranger to the gate. No one bothered the sleeping baby still strapped to the front of him.

"Maybe now we can get some answers out of him," Carson said.

Okay, sure, this dude started shouting, but he didn't seem dangerous to me. But I wasn't the boss, and no one seemed to care much for my opinion, so I pressed my lips together.

Before Carson could start his questioning, the stranger spoke. "Thank you for helping us."

Reaching over the baby's ridiculously full head of hair, Carson grabbed a hold of the man's shirt and shook him so hard his head hit the gate. "What's your goddamn problem? Are you some kind of goddamn idiot?"

"Carson, wait!" I had no idea why Carson was being so aggressive, but I wasn't gonna let him shut me up anymore, so I softened my voice and turned to the stranger instead. "Hey, what's your name?"

He tried to rub his head again before answering me. "Steven. Steve."

As if he'd snapped back to reality, he struggled

against the rope, and I could see him building to hysterics again. I couldn't help but feel sorry for the guy. I'd probably react the same way if I had asked for help and ended up tied up by a bunch of heavily armed, crazy-looking people.

"Look," Carson started, and his tone was firm. "You were acting like a lunatic out there on the street. You put us in danger. I had to get you inside, so you'd shut your goddamn mouth. You're tied up because the last guy I tried to help gave me this."

Carson pulled up his shirt to reveal a scar about the width of a blade. This revelation shocked everyone silent. After a short time, Steve broke the air.

"I was looking for help," Steve replied. "We've been walking for a while, and we're tired and out of food."

Equally exhausted, I breathed out a heavy sigh. I'd had just about enough of Carson, and couldn't deal with his shit anymore. I hoped he'd at least untie the poor guy. I didn't say anything else but went to go look for Brandon, so I could fall on my sword apologizing.

Not hard to find, I saw him through the back window smoking. Jordan had bandaged the arm I'd notched.

Orange flames lit his face, and he wavered a bit in front of them. He clutched a green glass bottle and poked at the fire with a stick he was holding, his cigarette in the same hand.

As suspected, he'd coerced Jordan into giving him one of the bottles, which was now a little less than half full. Who knows how full it was when he'd gotten it from Jordan? It didn't seem like that much time had passed.

Digging the toe of my boot into some gravel, I looked down, fully ready to be chastised. My stomach flipped.

"That was fucked, Nat," he said, moving closer to me.

"Which part?" I swallowed.

"Fucking everything. You sliced my arm, dude."

"Yeah, sorry about that." I tried to make my voice as casual as possible, unsure if it worked or not.

Brandon set the bottle down on a glass table with a sharp clink. He moved into my space and hovered there, blowing smoke off to one side.

I froze. My heart started thudding so hard I thought he might hear it.

What happened in the street showed me the items on my to-do list could conflict with one another. In trying to save Brandon, I'd put my own life in danger like a moron. Fuck.

"I shudder when I think about you sometimes." Brandon breathed the words onto me.

My breath caught in my throat, and I lost the ability to speak. I could feel my heart trying to beat straight out of my chest. When I thought about those times, when it'd been only just us, I remembered how soft he'd been with me, like I was some fragile thing and not someone who could drive a knife into a dead-not's head.

His good arm encircled my waist, and he pulled

me tight into him. He kissed me hard, like we were about to die, and every emotion I'd ever suppressed for him came bubbling back to the surface.

It took everything I had inside me to force myself to stop that kiss, that raw devouring, animalistic kiss full of fear and passion. Believe me, I didn't want to, but I knew my survival depended on it, and I finally pushed him away from me.

"Brandon, I . . . " I forgot how to use words but then coughed out, "I can't."

"Why? Because of Chloe?" He smirked.

"No. Wait . . . what? How did you know about that?"

Brandon, so drunk already, still held tight to his cigarette. He touched the tip of my nose like one would touch a child.

"Nat, Nat, Nat, I know you." His voice warbled with a playfulness.

He removed his finger, giggled, and then took a drag off his cigarette. Tears pricked the corners of my eyes. I hoped he wouldn't notice, perhaps too impaired by the booze he'd already downed.

"No, fuck Chloe," I whispered, looking away. "I mean, not literally. It's because it's you. It's always been you."

My eyes were hard on his in that moment, studying every centimeter of his face, pausing on his labret piercing and then gazing for a long time at his eyes.

Something shocked me. Something I'd never

noticed before in all the years I'd known him. Something new? Did this world cause it?

Underneath his left eyebrow the top of his eyelid sagged, making the crease harder to see on that eye. Why had I picked that moment to notice such a thing? More startling was that my right eyelid did the same thing. Our twin destinies were mapped on our faces. If we looked at each other, we mirrored one another. This had to be a mere coincidence, right? What had happened to both of us to weigh our eyes so heavily?

He picked up the liquor bottle, but before he could put it to his lips, I snatched it from him. I took a swig of it, coughing at the taste of the hard liquor. At that moment I wanted to finish every last drop, and I definitely didn't want to feel these fucking helpless feelings Brandon made me feel. A dopey lovesick child was less than useless in this world, so I decided I'd rather be numb.

He tried to take the bottle back, but I slapped his hand away, which only made him laugh. I finished it off, the alcohol burning my throat and making me feel a whole lot better and, to my surprise, less stupid.

I softly set the bottle on the ground near a pile of garbage. To be honest, I wanted to smash it into the wall, to burn with anger, to flip over tables, but there wasn't enough booze left in the world to drown my senses. And if I was too loud, dead-nots would come scratching at the wall surrounding our house.

"Nat—"

"What do you want me to say to you, Brandon?"

"You're being hella weird, Nat."

"You just fucking kissed me! Out of nowhere. You're the one being weird!"

I could feel the emotion rising in my throat like bile. I wanted to yell at him, to spew out all my feelings, but I didn't have time.

SEVEN

A NOISE, like an animal dying, sounded from inside the house, busting into our backyard drama. Brandon and I darted through the back door, weapons already in hand. The cry had come from Kelsey, and when we arrived, we saw her run through the front door.

"I swear I need a license to kill fucking dumbass people," Brandon said, shooting his eyes from the kitchen to the street outside.

I looked at the scene in front of me, trying to piece together what had happened while Brandon had kissed me out back. It appeared that Franklin had worked his magic on Carson and gotten him to untie Steve. Franklin cooed and tickled the giggling baby, bringing an eerie wave of joy fluttering around the tension in the room.

Standing in the open doorway, my eyes followed Kelsey past the gate and out into the street. When she turned, I saw tears streaming down her face. Looks like she'd met the baby for the first time.

While I'd been doing my detective work of what the fuck had just happened, Carson had already disappeared out the door after her, blade in one hand and 9mm in the other. Brandon, still armed, followed him.

Omar moved toward the door but was unarmed. Regaining some sense of the situation, I threw my weight into him to keep him from running outside after her. Even though Omar was taller than me, he was quite thin, and we both ended up tumbling over.

"Franklin! Jordan!" I cried for help.

Franklin passed the baby back to Steve, who'd gone wide-eyed at the commotion. Steve wrapped the baby, pressing the infant into his chest while Jordan and Franklin grabbed ahold of Omar, lifting him up and preventing him from moving any farther.

I jumped to my feet and pushed my hands into Omar's chest gently. "We'll get her."

It sounded like a promise, but words didn't hold much weight in this world. I jogged to catch up to Brandon and Carson, hoping I could help somehow.

Kelsey and I had never been great friends. On the rare occasion that I got her to talk to me, our conversation devolved into eating protein-rich foods versus the abuse veal calves suffer. Ugly whisper-yelling and name-calling ended that argument real quick. Disagreements aside, I didn't want anyone throwing themselves into the metaphorical dead-not infested waters.

Kelsey backed herself against a van which leaned forward onto two flat tires, and Carson pleaded with her, his voice a low hum. Brandon gripped his katana ready to slice into anything that came near them.

"Come on Kels," Carson pointed his gun toward the ground. "Come back inside."

"Shoot me Carson!" Kelsey's words shook the air, and some of the dead-nots shuffled toward us.

"Stop dicking around Carson. Drag her back by her fucking hair," Brandon hissed.

The moans of the dead-nots seemed to bounce against the van as they moved closer.

"No one wants this, Kelsey," I pleaded. "Please, come back."

Her brow narrowed, and her eyes almost disappeared. "I can't Natalie. I don't want to live anymore. You don't understand."

Kelsey leaned back against the van and slid downward like all her body weight was pulling her to the ground. Sitting lower back to the gap, she buried her head in her hands, immovable.

"Fuck," Brandon breathed, spitting.

Behind us, a holler shot our attention off Kelsey. I turned to see Omar running toward the van, arms outstretched as if he were ready to secure someone in a hug. He roused several dead-nots in his wake.

"Fuck," Brandon swore again.

"Omar, go back into the house! We'll bring her back. And shut up! You're drawing a lot of goddamn attention to yourself." Carson gave new meaning to the term "whisper-yelling."

Kelsey's blood-curdling scream was almost loud enough to shatter the van's windows. Out of view, a dead-not gripped her flesh with its teeth, pulling a chunk off her lower back. This, Omar's cries, and all the commotion around the situation crescendoed into a chilling melody. I couldn't even properly describe the sounds I heard, but this awful symphony was one I'd never forget.

The thing had been under the van. No one had seen it drag its legless torso closer and closer toward Kelsey until it finally tore her shirt and the skin from her back with its teeth. I wanted to say Kelsey herself hadn't known it was there, but, of course, I wasn't sure of that. Maybe she had.

Dropping to my knees near Kelsey, I shoved her aside and drove my Bowie knife into the skull of the one that had bit her. Kelsey's body moved like a pendulum for a bit but then slumped back against the van.

The situation went from bad to worse as the dead-nots now breathed their rotten breath too close for comfort. Brandon swung his katana, beheading the one closest to him. Carson drew his dagger as he kicked a dead-not to the ground. He stepped on its neck and drove the dagger deep into its skull. The dead-nots crowding around us now pulled their focus off Kelsey.

I crawled to her, and when I got there, jostled her body forward a bit to examine the bite. Not like it mattered.

My other hand hurt as my grip on my Bowie knife

caused my knuckles to go white. I didn't know what to do.

A dead-not was moving toward us now, swinging its arms at its potential meal. I shook the fog out of my head, jumped up, and buried my Bowie knife into its forehead.

They were coming in droves, rippling in from all directions. Why were there so much more of them than there'd been earlier?

"Natalie!" Carson barked at me; his voice was harsh, grating. "Help Omar get Kelsey up and get her back in the house!"

"Are you fucking kidding me?" Brandon yelled, way beyond whispering.

Brandon kicked a dead-not back, and it stumbled a bit. Dropping to his knee sideways, he swung his katana upwards and deep into the side of its throat, severing its head. Blood bubbled and sprayed out, covering Brandon with the splatter.

"No one gets left behind!" Carson shouted, extracting his blade from the back of a dead-not's head. No more trying to be quiet.

I helped Omar hoist Kelsey up. He threw her arm around his shoulders and jogged with her while she did a limp-jog back to the house. Blood had soaked her shirt crimson.

Everything moved in slow motion. As we trotted to the house, I assisted by trying to stab dead-nots in the brain. Kelsey erupted into big choking sobs, gasping in between the tears.

Brandon and Carson broke free, while we slow

runners served as an unintended distraction. They mad dashed in the direction of the house and caught us at the door.

"Chloe!" Carson flung the front door open, and his voice was clipped. "Jordan, Franklin, get your stuff. We got to move! They'll be surrounding this place soon. Omar, grab yours and Kelsey's stuff. I want you two in the SUV with me. Chloe? Chloe!"

As Carson shouted orders, everyone gathered whatever they could carry, moving faster than we ever had before. Unfortunately, we'd have to leave some stuff behind. Franklin's precious coffee came to mind at that moment.

In the beginning, we'd traveled light, one backpack per person. Two changes of clothes rolled tight, a stainless steel bottle for water, flashlights, matches or lighters which we pocketed every single time we found them, and one or two kinds of dry food for emergencies. Anything prepackaged and chocked full of preservatives worked.

Trying to stay pretty mobile meant we'd set up camp for a week at a time wherever we could. These days, it seemed we stayed longer in places we called "home" and thus had accumulated more and more things. Funny how even in a dead-not infested world, where survival was paramount, people still felt the need to have stuff.

Little by little, we secured a small caravan of vehicles, infinitely better than the previous method of cramming a bunch of people into one or two cars. So many vehicles still dotted the roads, either abandoned or still parked in garages. Sometimes we'd find the keys in the ignition or nearby. Occasionally, we'd siphon gas out of other cars, but other times we'd just switch vehicles.

The huge SUV, the head of our caravan, made a good dead-not plow. Even though the gas mileage was shit, it had lots of space. We kept a good stockpile of medical supplies, food, some blankets, and other survival type stuff in there. We never unpacked it when we set up camp because everything inside, like our first aid kit, was crucial. And we couldn't say when we'd have to bolt, much like our current predicament.

Carson disappeared, and when he returned, he dragged Chloe, his hand twisted around her shirt a little too hard. Okay, not really necessary. She rubbed her eyes as if she'd been asleep. He held her shoes in his other hand and threw them on the ground at her.

"What's happening?" She said, pulling her long hair back into a low ponytail.

"Put your goddamn shoes on. Let's go. We're leaving."

Chloe started to protest, but Carson had apparently decided to be this hardass dickhead today. He picked up her jacket and threw it in her face.

"Rude," I mumbled.

Not hearing me, Carson said, "Natalie, I'm taking Chloe, Omar, and Kelsey with me. Take your car and Brandon. Jordan and Franklin, can you take Steve and the baby in the other car?"

We didn't have much time left. The dead-nots had

already come scratching, shaking the fence around the house. To make matters worse, dusk had settled on our once sleepy neighborhood. Some people thought dead-nots were more prevalent at night. With night comes darkness. Full dark.

In cities there used to be a lot of light pollution which made nighttime not quite so dark. Since we lost power, night always fell darker than ever before. Prior to our shitty reality, that kind of full dark only existed deep in the countryside, where the moon was the only light in the world. Anyway, it wasn't that sunset brought them out any more than sunshine; it was just that visibility was significantly less at night, making it that much more dangerous.

We'd parked my car and the other car in the garage. We started loading up the vehicles with as much shit as we could as quickly as we could.

To get Carson, Chloe, Omar, and Kelsey into the SUV would be a bit more tricky as Carson had parked it in the driveway, where dead-nots now swarmed. Jordan and Franklin had grabbed some food and a few meager medical supplies from the house. When I glanced over, I saw Franklin trotting to the car, gripping the can of coffee in his hands.

Good for him, I thought.

Brandon and I collected all the weapons we could see strewn around the house. While doing so, I found the blanket Chloe and I had snuggled under. It seemed like an eternity since Steve and his baby had showed up, but it probably hadn't been more than an hour or so. I picked it up and passed it to Steve on my way to the car. Night would be super cold, and it was no fun being on the move, particularly in bad weather.

As I idled, I tapped my fingers on the steering wheel waiting for Brandon to open the garage door manually. When he did, Jordan peeled out of the driveway on the other side of the SUV, past the open gate into the street, hitting dead-nots on his way.

When Jordan started revving the engine, the dead-nots moved toward the loud noise. His car had served its purpose, acting as a distraction so the other four could get into the SUV.

The SUV had my car blocked in, so after Brandon had opened the garage door, he slid into the passenger seat of my car and we waited. While I was ready to go with the engine running, Brandon loaded a crossbow. He rolled down his window, and twisted his torso up and out and started picking off any dead-nots who approached.

Meanwhile, Jordan's car waited in the street, and Franklin fired at dead-not heads left and right with Jordan's pistol. Between Brandon and Franklin they'd carved a path of dead bodies which finally allowed Carson, Chloe, Omar and Kelsey to get into the SUV. It looked like we wouldn't be conserving ammo today.

Carson pulled the SUV out of the driveway crushing skulls as he backed over the dead-not-dead, now super dead. He sped ahead of Jordan's car. Brandon slipped his body back into my car, and had there been any dust to kick up, the dead-nots would have disappeared into it.

As night settled, leaving our headlights the only lights on the road, we followed Carson as always, putting our lives in his hands. Even if he didn't have a plan now, he'd make sure we survived.

No one could save Kelsey, but Carson would try to keep her comfortable for as long as he could before she got the head shot. He would also make sure that Omar could spend as much time with his dying sister as possible while she breathed human air. As hard as Carson was, he often said things that hinted he had a soft spot for true human love and affection. So mysterious.

Some time during the drive, Brandon reached his arm over and put his hand on my leg. When he did that, my heart slowed from its pounding inside my chest. His actions were so puzzling. One minute he was screaming about leaving the dying bitch, and the next he sought affection.

I wanted to pull the car over so he could fuck me in the back seat. All the shit that had happened today and that thought crept into my lusty animal brain.

For a moment, I forgot that we literally lived in hell on Earth, and my mind drifted back to the times when he and I would lie in his bed at night and talk before any of this shit ever happened.

———

I'd just gotten to his place and was ready to climb into bed with him. Earlier that night, I'd met up with some friends from high school, friends of mine that Brandon knew as well. Big city, small town, I guess.

"Jonesy was talking about you tonight," I said, shimmying out of my pants.

"He's different from the Jonesy I remember." Brandon was already reclined on his bed, shirtless as usual.

"He said you were sexy as fuck, scary smart, and he'll never get over you. Oh wait, no, that was me. I said that."

Brandon chuckled. "Stop. Jonesy though. Kinda broken."

A bit of sadness settled into me because Jonesy had always been the nicest guy. "He seemed a bit."

He flipped through TV channels as if unwilling to commit to anything. I sat down on the bed and leaned back on his stomach. A silence settled on us, so I changed the subject.

"I'd give my cyborg arm to be with you forever."

"Cyborg arm?" Brandon asked.

It worked. I now had his full attention, and he pulled me down to him.

"This story I'm reading. The main character has a cyborg arm." I breathed out small sigh of contentment with him this close to me. "I wish I had a cyborg arm."

"If it's anchored to your skeletal structure and you have leverage then you got a super strong arm. Don't know if I'd give that up."

"Good to know. But I'd give anything up for you," I said.

"Don't really know how to respond except I would definitely peel heads back for you."

A smile spread across my face. "I know. I'll let you know if I need heads peeled. Meanwhile, just fill me with all that knowledge in your big brain."

His hands were on me, but his head was still on the cyborg arm. "With enhanced mechanics on humans you do really need to think about weight and leverage though. Asimov knew this. It gets tricky."

"So it needs to be anchored to the skeleton."

"You need to reinforce the surrounding structure, in this case shoulder, neck, ribcage, and spine to accommodate the torque from said mechanicals with something lightweight and strong, kinda like smart-ish carbon fiber. Then you can have a super scintillated gel for the skin that automatically hardens like some kind of super cornstarch that withstands impacts and cuts."

"So it looks like a real arm? But what if I wanted the metal look? I think having a metal arm would show everyone you're a cyborg and give them cause not to fuck with you," I said.

"If you can solve the problem of the conductor material, well, really, you could make it look like anything as long as it's the the same mass."

"I like characters who walk up showing you that they're literally made o' metal. Like we know both Nebula and Gamora are enhanced, but Nebula fucking shows you right when she walks up."

"Mostly robit. Not robot," he said.

"I'm familiar with robits," I said. "And *Chobits*."

He smiled at the mention of the anime, and I matched his expression.

"You make me stupid smile. Like always," I said.

"That's what I'm here for."

"To make me smile?"

"Yup. You do the same to me."

We kinda sat in that moment for a bit.

"One day, I'm gonna get the fuck out of here. I just can't leave now, not without a solid plan." I forced the words out.

"Sorry," he said.

"That's life, I guess."

"No one gets out alive."

"True," I said.

He fell asleep before either of us could talk anymore about robots or leaving our shitty town. And I drifted off soon after.

————

I'd have to remember to write down that memory when we stopped. Those times were the happiest because neither one of us had to watch the window for dead-nots come scratching, and there'd never been another person I'd been able to sleep with so easily. And by sleep, I meant sleep. Not fuck.

In this moment, I didn't know where the drive was taking us, but I could think of no person I'd rather be with.

EIGHT

RAYS OF DAWN streamed from the horizon. My eyes burned. I'd been driving all night. Brandon had kept me awake talking about the time before. The TV shows or movies we'd watched together. Books we'd both read. Books I hadn't read that he summarized for me. Music we liked, which he sometimes sang to me almost comically.

He told me the plots of different comics whether I'd read them or not. He dropped a lot of knowledge about planes and his love of them. He could talk a person's ear off when he wanted to. This was the version of Brandon I loved most of all where his passions oozed into the light of day.

The poor visibility of night made it too dangerous to stop and switch drivers, so whoever had ended up behind the wheel when we dashed out of the house, like a drunken army, drove all night. The adrenaline that initially fueled me in the escape had kept me going, but now I'd felt woozy, overcome with exhaustion.

Listening to Brandon talk caused so many joyful and painful memories to bubble up to the surface, rising in my throat like bile. Even though he'd always been around in this dead-not infested world, we hadn't talked about us at all since I made him get in my car with only a backpack.

I'd worked so hard to put him out of my memory time and again, but my mind spun like a wheel. No matter what path it headed down, no matter what new lands it traversed, it would somehow end up back to him. Always.

"Why did you come get me?" He'd read my mind.

Creepy. The shock made me bite back my words at first. He knew I'd do anything for him.

"You know I'd do anything for you and give you anything and everything I could," I said.

But I'd told him and showed him this many times in many different ways, and no matter how many days passed from here on out, I'd continue to do so.

"And you know I'd kill anyone who ever hurt you," he said.

My heart twisted when he said this. I didn't say it out loud, but I thought about how oftentimes he'd been the one who'd hurt me the most.

"I had a car. You didn't." In another effort to be casual, I bit the insides of my cheeks, so I wouldn't choke on the tears threatening to fall.

When we were togetherish before The Collapse, Brandon had made it a point to fuck as many girls as he could. I stood on the sidelines of his life while these sexual endeavors occurred pretending I didn't know they were happening because dumbass Natalie, his faithful puppy, kept showing up for damn near everything.

Another time, he told me he didn't want to feel a certain way about another girl. Trying to bleed cool, I told him it was easy to not have feelings for someone —just don't. Like anything had ever been that easy, and I, for one, could probably benefit from my own advice.

How many times had I attempted to sound super casual, like I didn't care? I'd become an expert at being Brandon's buddy. His cool girl friend, never girlfriend. But now I could feel my heart trying to bust out of my chest. I rubbed my hand over it as if telling it to shut the fuck up.

Old wounds never died, and I knew then that old emotions would never fade, especially where Brandon was concerned. A single sweet word from him could drudge up my past feelings with so little effort. Then I'd drown, unable to turn those feelings off.

"You hurt me." My voice a low whisper with tears burning hot and then cold in the back of my eyes. "You know that? You were a real dick to me."

He stopped me with an apology. "Yeah . . . sorry. You're my girl, my badass girl."

I couldn't help but think that calling me his "girl" would not be the first, nor would it be the last broken promise.

He pulled one of my hands from the wheel, wrapping his around it. The number one word on my list, *survive*, seemed to hover in the road ahead of me as I realized I still loved him. I always had, but that love had nearly killed me so many times. I couldn't survive *and* love Brandon. Could I?

Number 2: Get Brandon back. How did I live without him for so long? A few years seemed like an eternity. Perhaps he'd never left me, always there in the deep recesses of my mind, whispering in my ear, shaping my destiny but ultimately bringing me back to him. Fucking Brandon.

I pulled my hand away from him and put it back on the wheel. I felt acid burning my throat, so I did the only thing I could think to do, I flashed my lights. Jordan received the message and flashed his lights, creating a ripple effect that stopped at the SUV in the front of the driving line. We had walkie-talkies at one point, but batteries had become scarce lately, and whenever we found them, we shoved them into flashlights.

While I had enjoyed being trapped in the car with Brandon with his hand on mine, stilling the air, nausea crept up as I realized the real prison was my mind, my emotions. I couldn't solve this problem, and these conflicting feelings threatened to have me doing some real stupid shit real soon.

Carson pulled the SUV into yet another cookie-cutter housing development, with no shortage of identical houses. He chose a street tucked away from the main road for safety. We followed.

When we stopped, everyone else got out of the vehicles cautiously, hands on weapons, except for me, who dashed out of the car to vomit in a bush.

The sun climbed slowly into the sky, and when I finished expelling the meager contents of my stomach into some overgrown shrubbery, I wiped my mouth and glanced around the area. Dead-nots didn't seem to be too prevalent here. Brandon's eyes darted from left to right, on guard.

But things here didn't look quite right. Several large obstructions one could easily hide behind dotted the area, cars parked in the endless driveways, large trees full of leaves, and fences galore. I thought I saw movement behind one of the vehicles. Still not feeling well, I shook it off as the remnants of nausea.

"How is everyone?" Carson asked.

No one answered, as obviously the question had been rhetorical. Considering the circumstances, it seemed like he didn't expect any answers either.

"Kelsey passed out. I have no idea if it was from pain, shock, or exhaustion. Omar is still in there with her. He's been up all night. And as expected, Chloe slept the entire time," Carson said, answering his own question.

Franklin gripped Jordan's shoulder.

"Steve and the baby are out too," Jordan said.

"We gotta figure this shit out," Brandon said.

We gotta get the fuck out of here, I thought with growing unease.

But I stayed silent, gripping my stomach as

everyone focused on staring at each other as if trying to telepathically form a plan.

One by one strangers appeared. As I saw them approach us, my stomach lurched again. The obstructions that I'd been glaring at before now faded into the background behind twenty people, all men, all large. A couple stepped in front of cars, others came from behind houses, several more walked toward us from behind high large cinder block walls. These movements were so bizarre, seeming to happen rapidly yet also in slow-motion. I blinked multiple times to make sure I hadn't gone completely nutty bananas.

They appeared with guns already drawn on us like extensions of their arms. Naturally, this forced all of us to pull out our weapons. We'd never seen another group of people larger than ours. I couldn't help but feel I'd put us in the wrong place at the wrong time.

What drew my attention most of all was the sound of clumping along the sidewalk as a woman, wearing bright red cowboy boots, strode toward us. She had the reddest hair I'd ever seen, and her pallid face was peppered with freckles. She had a tight grip on a shotgun, which she pointed directly at Carson.

I could see the visible tension snake through Brandon's body, and he had both hands on his katana ready to fight. Carson raised his arm in front of Brandon.

"What the hell is this?" Carson asked.

Guns drawn, the air felt stale, plagued by silence

in our immediate area. Off in the distance, I heard eerie noises: scratching, groaning, shuffling. We couldn't stay frozen in place like this for long before dead-nots dragged themselves our way.

"I'm gonna need you to lower your weapon, hon. And if you can have your team members do the same, I'd be much obliged." She smiled when she said that, and her voice was rich with Southern charm and oddly cheerful. "You're on our turf and mighty outnumbered."

My stomach somersaulted. No one even breathed. Our eyes fell on Carson as if begging for guidance. Carson lowered his weapon and put his other hand up.

"Fuck," Brandon swore under his breath.

The rest of us, even Brandon, followed suit.

The red-haired woman curled her finger at a burly Mexican dude standing in front of a car in the driveway where she'd planted her boots. Our cars seemed miles away but were a few steps from us, parked on the street in front of the house the red-haired woman had used as her stage.

"José c'mere," she said. "Collect their weapons."

"Listen lady, I don't know who you are or what you want, but we've got a sick girl here and a baby." Carson's voice took on a rare pleading tone, as if trying to generate sympathy.

The woman raised her eyebrows in what appeared to be surprise colored with genuine interest. "Well, don't keep 'em hidden on my account. Introduce us to the rest of your group. I'm always dyin' to meet new people."

She pushed Carson toward the vehicles while this José guy and two other big dudes relieved us of our guns and sharps. The even took the knife attached to the back of Brandon's belt. I thought about my Bowie knife still in my car, wedged between the center console and the seat. I couldn't bear to lose that precious thing and hoped they wouldn't search every crevice.

After that, they had us open the trunks of our cars and the back of the SUV. They took everything they could see. Meanwhile, the red-haired woman ordered Carson to get Steve and the baby up and out of Jordan's car. Then Chloe, Omar, and Kelsey filed out of the SUV. Now the ten of us stood there, disarmed and helpless, facing twenty of them with guns pointed right at our chests.

"I'm Marty," said the red-haired woman. "I'm not here to make enemies outta you, but I'm not lookin' for friends, either. Unfortunately, you've stumbled into our territory with what appears to be some hazardous cargo."

Marty nodded toward Kelsey, who'd grown even more pale and slightly grayish since I'd last looked at her. Omar was holding her up against him, but we all knew she didn't have much time left before she turned. She whimpered and winced with every movement.

"We don't leave people behind, especially our friends," Carson said, his voice a tense growl.

"Well," started Marty, "I guess therein lies the difference between you and me. I don't have friends. I have employees, people who're expendable, easily replaced. And any of them know that if they get bit, they get shot right in the head. I hope they're smart enough not to get bit. You see, it ain't ever a good idea to get too attached to any one person in this world. Our clocks are all tickin'."

I looked at Brandon, the only person I could ever say I was attached to in this world. His whole body had gone rigid, which scared me more than anything. For Brandon, angry meant dangerous.

Marty nodded at José, who now stood behind Kelsey. José grabbed a hold of Kelsey's hair, and she yelped as he forced her to her knees. Omar tried to move to help her, but another one of Marty's people restrained him.

The rest of us didn't move or speak. My breath caught in my throat. Though I didn't know these people, I knew what would happen next. After that, no clue. Sweat drenched my back, and beads formed on my forehead. I didn't want to watch, but I couldn't look away.

Kelsey's whole body trembled, and tears streamed down her cheeks. She knelt there on the icy ground, unable to do anything to veer from the path she'd put herself on. She never turned to face José, nor look at her brother.

José raised the gun to the back of her head in slow, almost calculated movements. He didn't fire though, keeping his eyes fixed on Marty. The corner of her mouth turned slightly upward as she nodded to José one final time. The shot that followed cut through the silence.

My skin crawled. Omar screamed like his flesh had been ripped from his body. I'd never heard a more painful scream in my life. He struggled with his captors, and they finally let him go at Marty's command. Omar crumpled to the ground on top of Kelsey's dead body.

Watching Omar's rivers of tears caused my eyes to well up too, and I looked over at Chloe, who looked like she'd been crying for a while. I had a powerful urge to reach out and enfold her hands in mine.

Time stopped, and Omar's chest heaved with sobs as he pulled Kelsey's body to him like he was trying to rouse her from a nap. I couldn't hold the tears in anymore.

Omar stood, and then, in one movement spun and lunged at José. José was caught off guard and dropped his gun in shock. They both hit the ground hard, José smacking his head on the asphalt. Omar put his hands around José's throat and started pushing José's head down and down until it met the road.

Marty took a few small steps toward Omar and José. She handed her shotgun to one of her men who was closest to the fight, and held her palm out while he handed her a different weapon, a handgun. Her features froze in a kind of sick calm. Fucking bizarre.

She raised the gun and shot Omar in the back, causing him to collapse on top of José. Dazed, José scrambled up, trying to push Omar's body off of him. Before he could shove Omar entirely off of him, Marty fired into his chest. I couldn't believe it. She'd just shot her own guy.

With a smile, Marty handed the gun back to the man who'd handed it to her. He walked to where Omar and José struggled to breathe through their gunshot wounds. He put bullets in each of their heads and then did the same for Kelsey, ensuring none of them would come back dead-not-dead.

NINE

A FEELING of sickness flooded every inch of me. If I'd had any food left in my stomach, I would have thrown up again.

Carson lunged at Marty but she nodded to a couple of her men, who restrained him before he reached her. He struggled violently until they brought him to the ground, pressing his face into the road. When they pulled him to his feet, he had bits of gravel hanging from cuts in his face.

After that, the rest of didn't fight as Marty's meatheads put us in handcuffs, legit handcuffs, and pushed us toward a van. They shoved us into the back. There were no seats, only the eight of us crowded on the floor of the van.

One of Marty's men drove while Marty sat in the passenger seat. She turned and smiled at Carson like she hadn't just murdered two of our people and one of her own. Sick and fucking scary.

"What's your name?" Her voice sounded like she was meeting someone at a bar for the first time.

He didn't answer but instead glared at her with a boiling hatred behind his eyes.

"It's okay, hon. You don't gotta answer me. I was askin' more out of a courtesy rather than a genuine interest." She dug her pinky nail into her back teeth before she spoke again. "Perhaps you think I'm mighty cruel."

Carson ground his teeth. "Don't call me 'hon.' Name's Carson."

"You got it, Carson. As I was sayin', I know you think I'm cruel, but I've got my employees to look out for. You put 'em in danger by bringin' an infected here. Moreover, one of your men attacked one a mine, so I did what I did to protect and defend my own. You woulda done the same if you were in my position."

Carson snorted out a laugh, making no effort to hide how he felt about this woman. I looked around the van. The rest of us were in various states. Brandon had balled his hands into tight fists. Franklin and Jordan huddled together, fear and worry painted on their features. I tried to keep my face as emotionless as I could, but it probably didn't look like it. Steve clutched the baby tightly, as if the infant would be ripped from him at any second.

Chloe rested her head on Carson's shoulder. At first, anger bubbled inside me. I swear nothing was ever worth her losing an ounce of beauty sleep over. Though as I looked at her more carefully, I noticed she was only pretending to be asleep, probably to avoid every aspect of such an uncomfortable situation. And, well, I couldn't blame her for that.

"I wouldn't have murdered innocent people." Carson spat the words out.

"You never have?" Marty asked, bringing the pitch of her voice up slightly.

"I've only killed the dead," Carson said.

Not dead, I thought.

The van coming to a stop cut their conversation short. When the doors opened, the sun shone bright and high in the sky, but the chill in the air bit at my face. Marty's men yanked us out of the van one at a time.

Looking at where we were shocked the fuck out of me. It was a police station which gave me more questions than answers. Were these people cops? Or former cops really, since cops didn't exist anymore.

Brandon positioned himself next to me, leaned in, and whispered in my ear. "I knew there was a reason I hated this bitch."

And despite our current predicament, I gave him a slight smirk.

Marty unlocked the doors, and her people led us inside the station. Inside, the room opened up into a pool of desks. They pushed us roughly down a set of stairs to the basement, where there was a row of cells.

"You've got to be fucking kidding me," Brandon said.

"No joke, hon," Marty said. "Welcome to your new home."

Although there was more than one, they shoved all of us into the same large cell. After locking the door, they took our cuffs off through the bars.

As soon as his hands were free, Brandon slammed one hand against the bars. "This is fucking bullshit!"

Marty only smiled and didn't respond. After they walked back up the stairs, we heard the heavy door close.

Carson sat down on a bench, put his head down, and then pulled his hands through his hair. He was thinking about something, often posing this way whenever he plunged deep into thought.

"Carson—"

"Nat, I'm trying to think," he said.

Again, I was no help to anyone, but unlike before, I couldn't just run away and hide. While being with these people had become the norm, without the freedom to take a break from them, I might just go crazy.

It felt like a lot of time had passed. I couldn't be sure because we were underground with no sunlight to go by. I could only guess based on the behavior of our group. Chloe was on a bench asleep or pretending to be again.

Jordan and Franklin sat shoulder-to-shoulder on the floor. Franklin slept on Jordan's shoulder while Jordan stroked his hair.

Steve rocked the baby who'd gotten fussier and fussier the more time had passed, probably because he'd been sitting in a soggy diaper for a while.

Brandon sat on the floor near the bars with his hand wrapped around one.

We heard the door open and footsteps coming down the stairs, but they weren't from Marty's trademark boots. A young girl appeared, maybe no more than twelve years old, carrying a basket and a liter of water. She didn't say anything but set the basket and water quickly near the bars, keeping a wide berth from Brandon and backing away even quicker.

"What is this?" Carson asked.

"I ain't supposed to talk to you," the girl said, starting back for the stairs. "But it's milk and diapers for the baby and some sandwiches for the rest of you."

I didn't wanna know where the milk had come from.

"You tell Marty, we don't want any of her poisoned food," Carson snapped.

The girl walked toward the cell, rolled her eyes, snatched a sandwich, and backed up to the wall again. She unwrapped it, took two big bites and made a show of swallowing, even sticking her tongue out to prove she'd actually eaten part of it. After that, she put the paper back on it and tossed it back in the basket.

"They ain't poisoned. I made them myself." She walked back toward the stairs again.

"Wait!" I said, unsure of where I was going with this.

She turned her head back to the cell, raising her eyebrows.

"What's your name?" I asked.

"Hazel." She turned and ascended the stairs.

"Thank you, Hazel," I said.

She didn't say anything else, and we heard the heavy door close.

"What the fuck was that?" Brandon asked.

"I dunno. She's just a kid and doesn't seem hard like Marty. We could use an ally here if we're ever gonna get out of this mess. Don't you think?"

I pulled the water bottle through the bars and then reached into the basket, picking up the baby bottle, diapers, and sandwiches to distribute them. Steve and the baby got their stuff first, and then I passed two sandwiches to Jordan, and set one by Chloe's head. Carson and Brandon got the last two whole sandwiches. That left me with the half-eaten sandwich.

"Sammiches," Brandon said with a hint of glee.

"How about that?" I grinned, looking inside the sandwich, "PB&J, your favorite."

We ate in silence. I watched Steve change and then feed the baby, who latched onto the bottle immediately. I felt really bad for that kid.

I didn't know what else happened that night because I passed out shortly after eating. Of course, not from anything fishy in the PB&J, but from the general exhaustion of the day.

That night I dreamt of Brandon and the real world. He smiled at me, and I couldn't count how many times I looked at his happy face in that dream.

We drove around, doing things like we'd done before all this stupid dead-not shit. We took naps together, drank at his favorite bar, kissed, and at night I crawled into bed with him, and after he fucked me, he held me tight. There were no walking nightmares in that dream world, neither in human nor dead-not form.

I woke to the awful clanging sound of Marty dragging a police baton across the bars. Even though Brandon had pushed his body close to mine during the night, I wanted to be anywhere else but here trapped in a cell by this maniac of a woman.

"Wakey, wakey," she said.

Carson and Brandon got to their feet quickly, and because Brandon's movement rattled me, I stood, too.

Carson didn't wait for Marty to talk. "How long are you going to keep us here?"

"Well," she said. "I always wanted pets. Daddy never let me have any, though. Too messy, he said, and I wouldn't take care of it properly. Y'all would make nice pets, especially your pretty girls."

"You know what would be nice? A boot to the face. From me to you," Brandon said.

"Aw, now that's not very nice at all," Marty said.

"Neither was slaughtering two of our friends." Carson pushed himself as close to the bars as he could.

"I thought you'd be over that by now, handsome." Marty smiled. "Perhaps you need a few more days to simmer down."

With that, she dragged the baton across the bars again, heading toward the stairs. She looked Carson directly in the eye, winked at him, and then turned to climb the stairs.

"Take it easy, Carson." Marty's words dripped out like honey.

Carson scowled, and Brandon kicked the bars.

It made my stomach turn every time she acted like she hadn't done a terrible thing, killing our friends and leaving us here to rot.

I suppose another day passed. We still had no concept of time, but out there the rising and setting of the sun didn't stop for anyone. Like before, eventually not one of us was left awake, all losing out to exhaustion once again.

Later, I awoke to Brandon nudging me. My back ached from the uncomfortable sleeping conditions, and I stretched, sitting upright next to him. He traced the outline of my hand before locking his fingers with mine.

"Why did you wake me up?" I whispered, though pretty grateful for his attention.

"Couldn't sleep. Nightmares," he said.

"I thought it was because you're a night owl." I teased.

"Vampire." He bumped me lightly with his shoulder.

"Wanna talk?" I asked.

"Yeah."

"Do you remember that book you read? *House of Leaves*?"

He paused for a second. "Yeah, best horror book in my world. That book scared the shit out of me."

"I remember," I said. "I was around then. Do you remember you called me up one night while you were reading it? Terrified, you asked me to come stay the night with you."

"You did." Not a question.

"I did," I echoed. "And then you told me about the book, parts you had read. I never wanted to read it after that. Just you describing what happened in that book made the hairs on the back of my neck stand up. And then, since you got it out of you, you were able to fall asleep. But then I was wide awake because I imagined everything you told me and was too scared to fall asleep."

I thought about the power he had over me, like with the book, the power of transference. He could make me feel the same way he did about anything, and in a negative vein, he could shift his fears over to me. Never in my life had I met anyone who affected me in such a way.

"I didn't know that," he said.

"I'm sure there are a lot of things you don't know about our time together. That night, I must have finally fallen asleep, though. I always loved sleeping next to you day or night; it didn't matter."

He wouldn't let me say anymore because he'd pulled me close to him, and his lips were on mine, hungry. This time, I didn't push him away. He always made me forget about this world. When he stopped kissing me, his arms circled me tighter.

"Good night, Natalie." His voice was soft and sweet.

"Good night, Brandon." Even though I must have looked foolish, I couldn't stop smiling.

My mind wandered back to times when my main concern was how to pay my bills, not how to cheat death every day. To tell the truth, I'd rather be there, and even though Brandon's arms were around me now, I definitely didn't wanna be trapped in this cell anymore.

TEN

HAZEL CLANGING on the bars with Marty's baton yanked me out of sleep, and I opened my eyes to the lights overhead burning into my retinas. I dug my palms into my eyes. In her other hand, she carried her signature food basket with a water bottle, and fresh diapers had been added. As usual, she quickly set them against the bars and backed away.

Doing anything without Carson's approval reeked of danger, but I thought I'd try something. I knelt down to get the contents out of the basket. While doing so, I looked directly at Hazel, trying to make my face as kind and unthreatening as possible.

"Hey, Hazel," I said.

"I ain't supposed to talk to you," came her standard response.

"I was just wondering, are you happy here? Are these people kind to you?"

"Marty is okay, I guess, but I'm waiting for Mama. Marty said Mama went out for a short while, but she'll be back any day now. Meantime, I have to help Marty and wait for Mama." Her words poured out.

I looked back at Carson with a sympathetic, pleading look in my eyes before turning back to Hazel. "Where did your mama go, Hazel?"

"She went to get supplies, but she'll be back any day. Marty says so," Hazel said, with a hint of sadness in her voice.

"I'm sure she will." I paused. "I hope to see you later, Hazel."

Hazel said nothing only climbed back up the steps, and within seconds we heard the familiar sound of the door closing.

"What was that all about, Nat?" Carson asked.

"I'm thinking Mama's not coming back," I said.

"Okay so . . . what is your endgame here?" Carson dragged his fingers through his hair.

"I think we might be able to convince Hazel to help us." I said, distributing the provisions.

"What makes you so sure?" Carson asked. "It's risky."

"I don't suppose anyone's got any other ideas." And then, lacing my voice with sarcasm, I turned to the bench. "Chloe?"

Chloe stirred slightly but didn't get up. Not that I thought she would anyway. She'd been doing nothing but sleeping since we'd been thrown in here, and I'd be lying if I said her tendency to ignore problems was really getting on my nerves.

"I think she might be onto something here, Carson," Franklin said.

"I'm with Franklin. It's worth a try," Jordan said.

Carson looked at Brandon, still needing more reassurance.

"Man, I just want the fuck out of here," Brandon said.

Bouncing the baby, who we'd only recently learned was named Akira, Steve contributed nothing. But I think we'd convinced Carson, and we set the plan into motion. Carson and Brandon tossed around ideas, but in the end Brandon won with fortitude.

The next time Hazel came down, Carson talked to her in a gentle and paternal voice with which I had never heard him speak.

"Hey Hazel," he said. "How are you doing? Your mama come back yet?"

"Mama ain't come back yet," Hazel said.

"Hazel, I was thinking if you could help us, we could help you find your mama." Carson said in hushed tones.

"But Marty said I shouldn't try to find Mama because Mama would come back on her own, but she's been gone a really long time." Hazel's face lit up, but she tried to hide it. "Could you really help me?"

"We absolutely could," he said. "But first, we need your help. Do you think you could get some things for us?"

Hazel nodded with an enthusiasm we hadn't seen before, and Carson ran down a list of items that he needed her to get. We planned to saw through the bars, a simple plan that would unfortunately take a long time. To do so, we needed dental floss, toothpaste, and salt, which were all things we assumed easy to come by. Things no one would really notice were missing. She disappeared pretty quickly after that.

"Do you think she can keep this on the down low Carson?" I asked.

"I think so. For her, there's something important at stake, the chance to see her mom," Carson said.

"Please tell me you're not using this little girl." Franklin frowned, his face colored with disapproval and judgment. "And that you do plan to help get her out of the clutches of that lunatic."

Before anyone could get another word out, we heard the door open once again, but it wasn't Hazel this time. Instead, Marty was back with three really large guys, one with a shotgun, following her down the stairs.

"Mornin' handsome." She looked straight at Carson.

Carson didn't respond, only narrowed his eyes at her.

"I'm gonna need y'all to back away from the bars," Marty said.

The large man with the shotgun hoisted it up and pointed it at us, and the other two men entered the cell. One grabbed Chloe off the bench, and the other pulled me up off the floor.

"What are you doing?" Carson said, seething.

"Ow, you're hurting me, you asshole," Chloe said.

"We're gonna borrow your girls for a minute," Marty said.

"The fuck you are." Brandon was already on his feet.

The man with the shotgun pointed it at Brandon now.

"Easy killer. Don't you worry one bit. We'll bring them back unharmed. Trust me no one wants any harm to come to these perfect young women you have here." Marty winked at Carson.

Chloe and I struggled against the grip of the men, which was dumb. These fuckers were huge, and I looked like a doll in their hands, and even though Chloe was tall, she definitely didn't have the strength to break free. Our efforts were in vain, and we had no choice but to let them take us. Marty locked the cell door, and after that both Carson and Brandon darted to the bars and gripped them tight.

"You touch one hair on their heads, Marty, I'll kill you myself!" Carson yelled after Marty as she walked up the steps.

The men shoved us up the stairs, and Marty followed. She didn't turn back to look at anyone in the cell, and the last sound any of us heard was the heavy door closing behind her.

Upstairs, I looked around. I didn't recognize anything on the main floor, which made me think I hadn't properly checked this place out when we were first brought here.

Several desks stood in the center, littered with debris. Behind those desks were a row of doors, some with windows, with numbers spray painted onto them. The paint had dried, leaving trails of red that looked like blood.

"Take the tall, leggy one into number 1, and this adorable little brunette into number 2," Marty said to the two men.

We wriggled against them, but to no avail. I looked at Chloe before they separated us. I saw fear and anger, equal to mine.

In number 2, the door lock clicked behind me. I didn't bother trying to open the door because I knew I wouldn't be leaving this room.

Marty definitely had a sick keeping-people-locked-up power trip going on here. Inside the room, everything looked sterile and gleaming white.

When I turned around, I saw a woman sitting on a swivel stool in front of a stirrup table like the ones at a gyno's office. I backed up against the door.

"Natalie is it?" The woman asked, her voice colored with kindness.

"Yeah, so . . . what the fuck is this?" I didn't remember telling anyone my name.

"My name is Dr. Porter. Can I ask you to have a seat?"

I firmly remained standing by the door. I didn't want to "have a seat."

Dr. Porter softened further. "Natalie, trust me, I am not here because I want to be. It would be best for both of us if you would sit and talk to me."

I had no reason to trust her, but her tone seemed genuine and soft, a stark contrast to Marty for sure.

Eyeing her sideways, I walked to the examination table, hopped up, and sat as she'd requested.

"I want to ask about your medical history. Have you had any surgeries?"

I told her about the miscarriage I had at twenty-one, and that I had to have a D&C to extract the tissue. She told me this information was good to know.

She then asked if my periods had been regular, and I explained that prior to this dead-not bullshit, my words exactly, I'd been on continuous birth control. When The Collapse happened, and I couldn't get birth control anymore, they seemed to regulate, albeit marred by spotting on both sides of the periods. Probably not a good sign, but since I wasn't a doctor, I kept that sidebar to myself. Dr. Porter made copious notes in a paper chart which I noticed had my name scrawled on it.

"Can you tell me when you had your last period?"

"Wish I could, Doc," I said.

"Care to venture a guess?"

"I don't fucking know! What is all this about?" I could feel the anger mixed with panic surging in me now.

"Do you mind if I examine you?" Dr. Porter remained calm, still speaking in quiet tones.

I raised an eyebrow. "What do you mean?"

"I'd like to check your cervical mucus and feel your cervix. It will help me determine where you are in your cycle."

"It will help me if you tell me what the fuck this is all about." I clamped my legs together.

"Natalie, unfortunately, I'm afraid I'm not at liberty to discuss what Marty has planned for you. They're monitoring me." Dr. Porter blew out a heavy breath and nodded at the door where a large, gross-looking guy gazed in through the high square window.

It looked like he'd just licked his lips. My whole body cringed.

Dr. Porter continued, "The only thing I can do is examine you and report back to Marty. You have two choices in the matter. Either you can permit me to examine you, or I will call Marty's men in here, and they will use whatever force necessary to hold you down while I do so. I don't enjoy doing the latter, but I will have to if you don't comply."

I considered the options she'd given me. Neither one of them sounded like something I wanted to do. However, she had a point that the latter choice didn't sound pleasant, so I hopped off the table, turned around and took off my underwear and pants. When I got back on the table, I laid back with my feet in the stirrups. I breathed a huge sigh of relief when she covered my exposed vagina with a towel, so the door creeper couldn't see anything.

Dr. Porter examined me, and just like I remembered it, it was super uncomfortable to have a doctor, let alone an unfamiliar one, stick their fingers inside me. Luckily, it didn't take long, and immediately thereafter she handed me a cup to pee into.

Of course, I got performance anxiety and couldn't go, so she gave me a warm juice box. I downed the whole thing in seconds. I drummed my fingers on my knees for a while. She sat writing more notes in the chart.

Finally, I told her I could probably do it. Looking away, she held the towel up, shielding me so I could go. That finished, she said I was free to put my clothes back on.

She dipped a stick into the urine, which was followed by more waiting.

"What's the verdict?" I asked after a few moments.

"Well, you're not pregnant," she said, scribbling more notes.

"I coulda told you that, Doc," I said.

She ignored me. "And it's either that your fertile window has just opened or is approaching."

"Great, fantastic, if I wanted kids— "

The purpose of the exam finally dawned on me, and something bubbled in my stomach. Marty wanted women to impregnate.

Why else would she be so interested in women's cycles? Why else would she take only me and Chloe? When I thought back to when Marty abducted our group, I now distinctly remember many men, but besides Marty herself I don't remember seeing a single woman.

For the first time, I looked, really looked at Dr. Porter. She was not young, maybe in her sixties. Marty also looked like an older woman. Not as old as

Dr. Porter maybe, but she certainly wasn't gonna be advertising skin cream. Fuck.

I don't think I could have kept the shock off my face if I'd tried. I didn't want to think about how Marty had intended to use me and Chloe for her bizarre plan, but I couldn't help it.

Obviously, she wanted us to be incubators. The room spun. I didn't want some disgusting sweaty goon on top of me. The very thought of it made my stomach flip.

"What now?" I felt the color drain from my face, and I couldn't seem to swallow the knot that had lodged itself in my throat.

"Now, I'll report back to Marty, and you'll likely go back to your cell while she makes a decision, but you probably don't have long . . . not long at all, I'm afraid."

"Fuck," I breathed.

Before I could get another word out, the bulky dude who'd initially shoved me in this room with Dr. Porter returned and dragged me back out into the main room. Unfortunately, what Dr. Porter had said hadn't turned out to be true. Instead, the dude shoved me into yet another room, and yet another door was locked behind me.

This room looked to be a bit more comfortable than the cell, as there was a small bed in the corner. A bed. Oh, fuck no. I felt some of the juice come up, burning my throat with acid, and I choked it back down.

I turned and beat on the door until my hands were

sore. I screamed as tears streaked down my face. No one answered. This room had no window, and no one opened the door at my cries. When my hands started to bruise and I went hoarse, I collapsed to the floor in a heap.

Though I was exhausted, I knew I couldn't dare fall asleep lest I be woken up by someone I didn't know on top of me. I couldn't think of a worse way to wake up. I wondered if Chloe had been put into a similar room like mine, and I felt sick for her.

Then I worried about what they had planned for our guys. Even though all of them were young enough to potentially have good healthy swimmers. It looked to me that Marty had enough dudes and no shortage of sperm.

I was lost without the security our group had offered me. And I would've given anything to see Brandon rip this door off its hinges. Every piece of the semi-security I had before was now replaced by fear, apprehension, and pure terror.

Marty made the dead-nots seem like a far less frightening foe. At least we mostly understood their motivation: to feed. Her motivations remained a mystery. I didn't want to cry again, but also really wanted to cry again. I'd never felt more helpless in all my short life.

ELEVEN

THE SOUNDS of gunshots and yelling outside the door yanked me out of sleep. Scrambling up, I cursed myself for dozing off.

Though muffled, I recognized Marty's distinct voice almost right outside my door. She was yelling at someone to help her "get this girl the fuck out of here!" Still locked in this room, I knew she couldn't be talking about me. She meant Chloe, and what happened next confirmed that suspicion. Chloe screamed. But her scream trailed off, and I heard several obscured voices I didn't recognize.

Then, after what seemed like an eternity, someone moved close to my door, and the next voice was clearly Hazel's. "She's here, Mama."

The door opened from the other side, and in the doorway stood a woman shorter than me with slicked back hair. She had several weapons strapped to her and wore dusty jeans and combat gear. Hazel peeked out from behind her.

"No time for introductions. I'll explain everything later," Hazel's mama said. "Some of my people are releasing your friends. You should come with me now."

When I emerged from the room, I saw the aftermath of the earlier commotion. Bodies were strewn about the police station, peppered with either gunshot wounds or clear stab marks. They were all men, Marty's men, to be specific.

I don't trust people. I don't. But this woman had slaughtered a great number of my captors and was, as we spoke, freeing my friends. I felt inclined to trust her more than I had trusted others in the past, so I followed "Mama" without a hint of protest. And when I did, relief washed over me.

Outside, the sun blinded me, but Hazel grabbed my hand and walked me to what looked like the outline of a pickup truck where a familiar hand grabbed mine, pulling me up into the truck bed.

Feeling the tears behind my eyes, I latched onto Brandon, and he tugged me to him, gripping me in the tightest hug. It felt like we hadn't seen each other in years. He smoothed back my hair, and I crushed my face into his chest.

Hazel's mama started yelling orders that we had to "get out of here and quickly" as the noise had roused several dead-nots, who'd already dragged their way toward the police station. But I was okay, and I hadn't felt this safe in a while. "Mama" seemed to know what she was doing.

I closed my eyes hard and listened to the dead-nots shuffling toward us in droves, followed by the sounds of our tires speeding away. Moans faded into the wind.

My eyes didn't stay closed for long because I felt someone nudging me. When I opened them, they'd adjusted to the light a little bit, but it was still blindingly bright with the sun ablaze over our heads. The nudger was Carson, who looked serious but worried.

"Nat . . . " He paused for a long time before continuing. "Did you see what happened to Chloe?"

I looked around for the first time. Chloe wasn't in the pickup truck with us. How fucking stupid that I hadn't noticed it before. Our group had been cut down again. Only Brandon, Carson, Jordan, and Franklin remained. Chloe wasn't here neither was Steve and baby Akira.

"Carson . . . Marty . . . I think she . . . " I couldn't get the words out.

Hazel's mama, who had the small window behind the bench seat of the pickup truck open, had been listening to us and took over before I could say anything else. "Marty took her, threatened to kill her if we didn't let her take your girl."

"Goddammit!" Carson spat.

"Did you see a man with a baby?" Franklin asked her.

"I didn't see anyone with a baby, no one," Hazel's mama answered.

"What happened to Steve and the baby?" I asked Franklin.

"His name's Akira." Franklin reminded me. "And

we don't know. Marty took them out of the cell shortly after she took you and Chloe."

I swallowed hard. So Chloe was with Marty. But because she was valuable to Marty, I knew she was still alive. She must've also deemed Steve and Akira to have some value, but I couldn't guess what. This led me to believe they were still alive too.

I felt beyond guilty for being rescued while my friends were still being held prisoner by that awful woman. Even though it wasn't my fault that they were taken, I still felt like shit. Like why was I rescued and not Chloe?

So hung up on Brandon, I'd hardly paid much attention to Chloe lately. But I knew myself better than anyone. I'd always been like this, easily distracted, especially when someone was hyper focused on me.

Since we split, Chloe hadn't shown much interest in me either, which was fair, but these days Brandon tossed affection at me every chance he got. It wasn't a complaint. I loved it, and he'd always had that effect on me. He could make me forget about the weight of the world, but I still felt like a jerk that I hadn't cared enough about someone who I'd been close to not too long ago.

We drove for a long time down some dusty roads. Not fun in a pickup truck, but remembering the alternatives, it wasn't even half as shitty as what we'd faced already.

I blinked in surprise when we finally pulled up to one of those big box warehouse club stores. Why hadn't we thought of that before? With the exits secured, it would be a near impenetrable fortress, keeping its inhabitants safe from dead-nots and mortal foes alike.

Not only that, but it also had a solid supply of food as well as clothes. Back when there were still ads, I remember them screaming about modern comforts like furniture, even massage chairs which were still comfortable despite a lack of electricity.

The truck moved through the parking lot past the front entrance of the store, which looked like garage doors. They'd been shut tight and didn't appear to be damaged. This warehouse store had no windows that I could see. The pickup truck and the other vehicles that followed pulled around to the back of the store, parked, and everyone jumped out.

"Mama" took Hazel's hand, leading us to a single door, which she distinctly knocked on until it opened. The woman, who opened it, nodded at her and eyed the rest of us but did not stop us from entering the building.

Inside the warehouse store, we looked around wide-eyed. Looking like a kid on Christmas, Brandon abandoned us to run straight to the alcohol. Meanwhile, I followed Carson, who was following Hazel's mama, and Jordan and Franklin excused themselves saying they wanted to sit somewhere comfortable. I didn't blame them. They'd been in a jail cell for who knows how long and then loaded into the back of a pickup truck. A bit of comfort would have been on anyone's mind.

A boy, who was about thirteen or fourteen, ran up to meet Hazel's mama and jumped around when he saw that she had Hazel with her.

"Hazel!"

"Bobby!"

They hugged.

Hazel's mama explained that Bobby was Hazel's older brother. Waving to us, Hazel quickly ran off with him to meet a small group of children who screamed and shouted upon seeing her return.

"I suppose now is as good a time as any to introduce myself. As I'm sure you've figured, I'm Hazel and Bobby's mama, but those who I've not taken a hand in creating call me Alice."

"Carson," he said, vaguely gesturing to himself. "And this is Natalie. Brandon is the one knee-deep in the alcohol over there, and Jordan and Franklin are the two who've collapsed on those easy chairs."

I gave half a wave, followed by a poor attempt at a smile.

Alice led us to a huge dining table, which looked like their base of operations. Maps littered the table; some were actual printed maps while others were crude, hand drawn. She gestured for us to sit down.

"Hazel and I, along with a couple of other women, were ambushed by Marty and her men a while back when we were out looking for supplies. At first they locked us in a cell like you guys. Not too long after that, we, me and the other women, were taken to her doctors and examined like you and Chloe were.

"Marty explained to us her particularly crazy

notion that God had chosen her to do 'His work.' In this scenario, 'His work' meant repopulation. Perhaps you've noticed Marty is seriously lacking young fertile women in her group, so you can imagine how overjoyed she was to stumble upon a group of women like us. Hazel's just short of eleven. No period yet, which was really lucky, so Marty put her to work while the rest of us were prepared to be impregnated.

"The doctors examined us for signs that one or all of us might be within a window to conceive, and all of us were tested for pregnancy. Because I came with Hazel and was the only mother in the group she captured, I, like your friend Steve, had proof of my fertility. Therefore, I became a high priority to Marty."

A lump formed in my throat that I couldn't swallow no matter how hard I tried.

"Like you Natalie, I was put in one of the White Rooms, as we called them. I'm not young like you, but not so old either, so I fit Marty's criteria. Marty didn't give any of us a choice. I couldn't be sure, but I think that we were her lab rats, her test subjects. Since she had never tried this before us, I don't think she knew what she was doing to be honest. When I figured out what the exam was about, I lied to the doctor. I told her that I had just had my period, which would mean that I would be fertile soon.

"The truth was that it had actually been weeks. Not only that, but I withheld other information about my medical history. Because I had lied, I figured that one of her slimy guys would be in to have his way with me soon enough. I was right, and luckily for me she sent in some weaselly, skinny, trashy-looking dickhead, as at that time she hadn't rounded up the Spartan army you encountered.

"What he didn't know was that I had spent the time waiting for him by ripping into the mattress I was sleeping on. It took me a while to find a weak enough point to rip with my fingernails, but when I did I was able to extract a coil from the old box spring. I kept it hidden under the mattress until I needed it, and that was right when the rapist walked in.

"Marty sent this idiot in with a firearm. He came in and pointed the gun at me with his puffed up chest. With a false sense of power, he ordered me to undress. I did what he said, and then crawled back into the bed, covered myself, and acted terrified. I was scared, sure, but not as frightened as I was acting because I knew I was about to stab him in the throat.

"I knew this moron couldn't rape me while holding a gun, and he would put it down soon enough. He did, fumbling out of his clothes and putting them and the gun under his hat on the table in the far corner of the room.

"Before he even touched me, I knew he had to be thinking about how lucky he was, but the distraction was good. I wanted him thinking about what he was going to do to me, so he couldn't even imagine what I was about to do to him.

"He crawled into the bed and got on top of me, and if I was going to get out of this alive, I had to wait until he was completely distracted by what he had intended to do to me. I played the weak girl. Even threw in a few whines for good measure."

My knuckles went white listening to her recount what had happened.

"He grabbed my hair and slapped my face. But my hands were free, and I reached under the mattress and pulled out the spring, which I had crudely shaped into a pointed weapon. I didn't even think, just stabbed and stabbed into his neck repeatedly until I was certain I had hit his carotid artery. He died almost instantly.

"Surprisingly, the whole thing had been relatively quiet, but I soon found out that it was nighttime and there wasn't anyone awake to hear it anyway. I grabbed his clothes, hat, and keys and, of course, the weapon. A quick glance could've fool anyone into thinking it was him exiting the room.

"I slipped out of there undetected and finally made it back here. When I got you guys out, my goal was obviously to free Hazel, but Marty still has some of my women. I'd thought they would be in the police station but when we ambushed it, we found only Hazel and you guys, so we came back here to regroup."

When she finished, I could finally breathe again.

Alice showed us the large map of the city in the center of the table, pointing to a location marked in blue.

"We're here. The police station is here." She moved her finger to a location marked with a red X.

I noticed several other areas on the map marked with yellow.

"We think she has the women in one of these three places, but our best guess is here." Alice pointed to Our Lady of Perpetual Sacrifice Hospital labeled with a question mark over it.

"We want to help," Carson said. "We want our people back, too. We don't leave anyone behind."

"That's what I was hoping you'd say," Alice said. "Now go on. Eat and rest. We'll set out in a day or two after you've recharged."

TWELVE

WHEN MARTY HAD TAKEN US, we'd lost everything. I couldn't even think about my Bowie knife, so I lamented the loss of my unicorn notebook instead. The warehouse store had plenty to choose from, so I picked one with a gray kitten on it, eager to recreate what I'd lost.

After securing a new notebook, I rummaged around the bedding area, looking for the comfiest, coziest pillows and blankets I could find. I loaded all of them into a deep red wagon I'd pulled from another part of the store, creating a rolling mountain of relaxation. Then, I went looking for Brandon. As expected, I spotted him drowning in alcohol, but still incredibly coherent.

"Hey Natalie Nats," he said in a singsong voice when he saw me.

"Hey yourself. Wanna find some place to chill?" I nodded at my comfort wagon with a smirk.

He smiled, which I took as a yes, and we went to

seek out a place somewhere in this giant warehouse where we could hide out. We found a quiet spot at the far end of the store. With no one around this area, Brandon pulled up some empty palettes to make a crude wall under one of the shelves.

Covering the floor with blankets and pillows gave us our own little fort. The only thing missing were twinkle lights. Too bad for lack of electricity.

Brandon giggled and pulled from his back pocket a small strand of lights shaped like margarita glasses attached to a battery box, and when he flipped the switch, they lit up. Unbelievable. He wove them through the shelf above us and the nook glowed with warm amber and green lights. I looked up, mesmerized.

I only snapped back to reality when he crouched down behind me and ran his hands down my arms, enveloping me in a backwards hug.

"Thought I'd lost you," he said, his soft breath brushing the top of my ear.

Normally I'd melt into his arms, but I just couldn't. I froze.

"I can't do this anymore," I whispered.

"What?"

"This . . . us. Whatever this 'us' is. I can't keep pretending that you mean nothing to me and that I don't care when, in actuality, you're everything to me. You're all I care about, way more than any of this shit. You're all I have in this fucked up world. You're all I've ever had . . . even before the world was fucked." I exhaled all my frustration, and I had to take several breaths before I could continue. "Is this gonna be like it was before, Brandon? What the fuck are we?"

I hated listening to myself like this. I sounded stupid and weak. Brandon would always do whatever he wanted. He would never be mine, no matter how much I cried or begged for his love. Weak. Weak. Fucking weak. Brandon always made me weak.

It didn't benefit anyone to be weak in this world even if wonderful things such as love, devotion, adoration, and gratitude caused that weakness. However weak I was, I needed answers, and I needed them right now.

"I can't remember what happened exactly, why you finally stopped talking to me the last time, the final time. Can you remember?"

"Not exactly," he said, as if thinking out loud. "I think I was working, just working all the time?"

"Can you tell me *why*?"

"Why, what?"

"Why I was never good enough for you," I choked out, trying to hold back tears. "I always thought you were so cool."

"I do believe it was mostly smoke . . . lots of smoke and mirrors. I ain't that cool. Shit, I wasn't even that cool before. But I hated myself back then, and I hated that you hated yourself." He leaned back on a pillow.

The revelation that Brandon never thought as highly of himself as I thought of him cut me to the core. He told me once before all this shit happened that he wasn't "a rockstar or a huge catch" and considered himself "a cynical alcoholic with a healthy dose of realism."

He didn't have "rainbows or comforting ways for anyone." And he thought he was "like two steps away from being a terrorist in the government's eyes."

But what he said about *me* hit me harder than anything else. He was right. I had hated myself a lot in the five years we spent together.

"It doesn't help one's self-esteem to be deemed good enough to fuck but not good enough for anything else," I mumbled.

He continued, "I never got it, why you hated yourself so much. I thought you were fucking great, but I knew if we got together, I'd just cheat on you. I wanted to have sex with a lot of girls. I was a slut. And I did have sex with a lot of girls."

The pain of our past cut through me. "It wrecked me, Brandon. You wrecked me."

"Don't worry. Karma got me. I met a sociopath, and she wrecked me so . . . " He trailed off, leaving his sociopathic ex-girlfriend a mystery, one I didn't care to unravel. "I used to think I was a sociopath until I met one. Sociopaths lack empathy, and I got that, so definitely not a sociopath."

We sat stewing in the awkward silence that permeated our fort until he spoke up again. "I feel like this is part of a 12-Step Program where you gotta apologize to all the people you wronged. I hope that gave you some closure."

I coughed out a little laugh, not knowing what to

do or say next. I could never hate him, no matter what. If he continued to break my heart from now until the end of time, I would always run back to him.

However things turned out, how could I hate someone who practically stitched together the fabric of my life? Impossible. The person who existed in that moment, and the person I'd always be, was because he blew into my life like a tornado, taking all of me and swirling it up into him.

I can't even remember who I was before he came into my life. What kind of things did I like? Who was I? An empty notebook? Pages and pages for him to fill? Why couldn't I remember a life before Brandon?

The bigger question was did I want a life without him in whatever form it came in? The easy answer was no. Never. I never wanted to imagine a life without him no matter what.

But honestly, I was scared. Why? Brandon had been known "to go nuclear," a phrase he himself coined for his behavior, which meant that he'd drop everyone in his life to avoid unnecessary drama. He'd bounce. When Brandon bounced, the emptiness he left behind was inexpressible. I can only liken it to knowing everything about a certain subject and waking up one day to find a brain empty of all knowledge of said subject. That's how it felt. A nameless, gaping void. A black hole.

But we'd been with Carson and Company for what seemed like a long time. He hadn't disappeared, but even if that were true now didn't mean he couldn't make it untrue at any time. A future disappearance loomed around every corner.

I didn't want to reconcile, to finally forgive him, only for him to be gone one morning when I woke up. The feeling of impending doom suffocated me, and if I thought about it too long, I couldn't breathe.

It was a paradox. I couldn't imagine being without Brandon, yet it was impossible to be with him. A walking catch-22. Neither with nor without.

I bit my tongue for fear of cracking the thin ice I, and everyone else, always walked on around him. Once that metaphorical ice cracked, I'd fall into freezing waters, and that would be the end of me.

I couldn't talk about that now, so I decided on a safer topic instead. "I know about such cool shit because of you."

"Doubtful," he said. "How do you know you wouldn't have found all that stuff yourself? You were already headed in that direction. If anything, I just exposed you earlier."

My argument, which I posed again now, had been the book. *The Snow Queen*. It happened as if organic. Me sitting on his bed. Him digging in his closet until he handed me *The Snow Queen*, as if demanding I read it. So I had no choice. I *had* to read it.

It ended up becoming my favorite book, one I'd carry around a dead-not wasteland if I could ever find another copy.

But when he gave it to me, it hadn't been a super known book, a rare and obscure space opera, and something I don't think I ever would've found. So I couldn't believe that I could've, by some accident, ever stumbled upon it myself.

No, Brandon is without a doubt responsible for shaping Natalie, which all started when he handed me that book in the shadows of his room in that house where I used to have to bang on his window, not the front door, if I wanted in.

"I'm lucky my mom got me stoked on reading. All of my knowledge of my physical surroundings comes from books. But you're the only one who seems to understand the books I read," he said. "I mean, *actually* understand."

I felt my face burn. "You're the only one I ever took book recommendations from. I mean it. Unless your name is Brandon, I don't take book recs from you."

He smiled. "Every time you say it, I feel so warm inside but also in my toes."

I couldn't help but return his smile. He always navigated the situation out of dangerous waters with his magical Brandon charm.

But the pain of the past had been seared into me. It restrained me, keeping me from moving forward, forever scarred by the wounds he'd left. Even though I knew it, and he knew it too, it seemed like we always needed to remind each other that those wounds ran deep. When he saw the seriousness return to my face, he changed his expression to match mine.

Brandon took one of my hands in his. "I was, and

am, and will always be quite fond of you. But I really was a dick to you."

"I know, Brandon." Tears welled in my eyes, and I had to turn my head away. "I think that I was lucky, at least. Because even though you were a dick and I knew that, I still got to see a part of you that I know most people never did and never will."

"I really can't say one way or the other on that, but thank you. It means worlds to me." He paused before continuing. "I hate doing this because I feel like as soon as you say you're sorry for something it's kinda like opening the floodgates and giving that person the opportunity to let loose all of the things that've ever bothered them about you. At least I'm trying to make amends. Better late than never, I guess. But you should know there are not many people I would like to try and repair bridges with."

I doubted that there were many people left in this world with whom we could repair said bridges. It's funny how a world in chaos can put aside the necessities of mending broken relationships. Brandon and I never tried to seriously fix things because that was never our main concern.

We'd been so focused on survival day in and day out that repairing the hurt of the past didn't matter. Yet, I always told myself that if I ever got a hold of Brandon again, I would grip tight to him until my knuckles bled and never let go. But since he'd been back in my life, I hadn't held onto him very tightly at all.

Brandon got to his knees and looked at me with a

half-cocked so sure-of-himself smile that penetrated deep into my soul, shattering my resolve. He knew it too. All my fear and worry melted into lust. I wanted all of our history, all this need for remedy coupled with the sour memories, to be erased by our bodies pressed together.

I got up off the floor and crashed so hard into an embrace with him I almost knocked us both over. If anything, it meant I could touch him, so I didn't have to look at him as he devoured everything about me with a single look.

Without warning, Brandon broke our embrace and grinned at me like a cat with a feather caught in his teeth. He reached around and pulled a book from behind him. Before he moved his hand off of the cover, I recognized it. *Hyperion*. My eyes sparkled with tears.

"There's tons of books in here, but this one . . . I know you remember this one. Read it to me. I like when you do the voices," Brandon said.

He nestled himself into our makeshift blanket fort and held his arms out for me to join him, and I secured myself close to his body. The lights twinkled above us, and I read until we fell asleep in each other's arms.

I awoke in the middle of the night with a ridiculous urge to pee, and I wondered if people were just filling the toilets here or what. The smell from the bathrooms gave it away. The women's side was spray painted with a number one and the men's a number two.

On my way back to the fort, I spotted Jordan sitting in a recliner reading by flashlight. I figured I'd just breeze by him.

"I apologize, Natalie," he said.

Furrowing my brow, I turned back to him. "What?"

"It seems that in my sleeplessness, I happened upon your conversation with Brandon, and I do admit I overheard."

"So?" I put my hands on my hips.

"Historically speaking the toxic male ego has been romanticized for eons." Jordan folded his book on his lap.

"What's your point? Assuming you have one."

"My favorite novel is *Pride & Prejudice*. It depicts a man who is aloof, inconsiderate, and arrogant, but he can also be a kind and generous person, extremely loyal to his loved ones. He would do anything to protect them. When a man like this opens up to a woman, it can make her feel special, like she was specifically chosen as someone to whom he can expose his true self. It must be said then that the woman feels a sense of true love therein, and thus she is willing to tolerate his abhorrent behavior. Does this sound like anyone we know?"

"Fuck you, Jordan."

"Pardon me?"

"I said, fuck you. You overhear one conversation between me and Brandon and suddenly you're an expert on our relationship."

Before he could retort, I stormed of, giving him the finger as I walked away.

My anger cooled as soon as I peeled back the blanket door of the fort. Brandon looked so peaceful there asleep, and I wanted to absorb some of that calm so I could forget about what Jordan had just said.

I slid in beside him, and his arms went around me so effortlessly. He pressed a kiss to my forehead, wrapping his arms around me tighter.

One time Brandon told me that my memories were "skewed," the exact word he used, but I refused to believe that. I knew there were two Brandon's back then, and I knew the two of him very well.

My memories of the five years I spent with him were not always kind, but the ones that were had allowed me to throw together some semblance of happiness. I wanted to cling to that, however small it was.

I chose not to dwell on the tears shed because of him, the countless times he shoved me out of his life, the girls he fucked instead of me, who I truly was to him. I wanted to remember the Brandon who was sweet and loving. The one who gave me toys, trinkets, and books, the one who held me close to him as we slept, the one who not only invited me into his whole world but who also made me fall in love with it and with him, too.

The past flowed into the present. I never thought he'd ever have his arms around me again. Grinning up into the twinkle of the lights, I felt overcome with a feeling I'd not known in years. This moment was enough.

He didn't have to fuck me, though honestly, I'd welcome that, too. He just had to hold me like this, like he'd done before all those years ago.

Maybe it didn't check off "get Brandon back," but I felt like I could survive like this. After all, I had before.

THIRTEEN

PEEKING out of the blanket door of our fort in the morning, I saw people had already gathered around Alice's mission control table at the other end of the store.

Damn. I couldn't stay camped out in here with Brandon's arms around me all day. We had plans to make, people to rescue.

Franklin made wild gestures while holding a mint green mug, coffee if I had to guess. I smiled.

"I think we better make an appearance." I tossed Brandon his t-shirt, which he'd taken off during the night.

He mumbled incoherently while putting the shirt on. Then we crawled out of the blanket fort and made our way to where everyone had gathered around the table.

"Morning sleepy heads." Franklin gave me a wink.

I don't know what he thought had transpired last

night, but I didn't have time to ask as he wrapped an arm around my shoulders.

"Nat, my god, they have almond milk here and artificial sweetener. It's like heaven." Franklin gripped my shoulder and showed me his large steaming mug of coffee.

Couldn't argue with the smell. It perked me right up, and I smiled at Franklin, patting his hand.

"Carson has been filling me in this morning on how you guys have been doing things," Alice said. "I like the buddy system your group has been using, and we would like to use it for this rescue mission. So with the absence of some of the buddies namely Chloe, we've done some shuffling around. I'll pair up with Carson. Jordan and Franklin, I want you with two of my ladies: Sarah and Naomi. Brandon and Natalie, you two okay to be buddies?"

"I don't see why not." I don't know why she asked us and no one else the same question, but maybe she'd already checked with the others while Brandon and I were still hiding out early this morning.

"We've got brand new weapons for you as long as you don't mind that they've been used before." Alice pointed to a woman with a jet-black ponytail. "If you follow Sarah, she'll get you outfitted with knives and firearms, and some serious combat gear."

"Dope," Brandon said.

"All of Marty's men are expendable, you got me?" Alice's tone clouded with a dark seriousness.

"We 100% get you," Carson said. "I'd like to kill her myself."

"Get in line," Alice said. "Go on, get suited up."

Carson, Brandon, Jordan, Franklin, and I followed this dark-haired chick Alice had called Sarah.

It pained me to think about only the five of us following her. Didn't there used to be ten? Wasn't that something like last week? Time had gotten all fucked up inside my head. It had to have been longer than a week, right? Why didn't time ever seem to make any sense these days?

Sarah led us to a shelf that had been cleared of products, now showcasing an array of weapons. Various handguns, two shotguns, a couple of automatic weapons, and several pointy objects had been spread across the shelves.

"Alice used to work at a weapons museum," Sarah explained. "When everything went to hell, she cleaned it out. She's got a lot of unusual goodies here."

Scanning my eyes over the sharps, I'd almost missed it. In the back, in its case, was my Bowie knife. Not just any Bowie knife, *my* Bowie knife.

"Where did you get this?" I asked Sarah, picking up the knife.

"You tell me where I got it, since you seem to recognize it," Sarah said with a smirk.

"You found it wedged in between the seat and the center console of a four-door black sedan, didn't you?"

"That's correct. I think you've found your long, lost friend," she said.

I ran my fingers over the Bowie knife. I couldn't

believe they'd recovered it. I thought I'd never see this again. I unsheathed and sheathed it several times trying to make sure it was real.

Brandon looked impressed as he picked up a Japanese blade shorter than a katana. "Shit, this is a wakizashi, popular in old timey Japan."

"This one is from the museum," Sarah said. "Most of these arms broke fast, considering when and how they were made. Alice said this one was remade with Toledo steel, which allowed it to withstand the test of time."

"Samurai usually wore a wakizashi with a katana. It told people he was a samurai and not one with whom to fuck. Wakizashi was perfect for close combat and beheadings. Ergo, the blade you want for times like these. Also, I have a hankering to slice open some dead-not stomachs. Some kind of reverse seppuku. You're familiar with seppuku, Nat, right?" Practically drooling, Brandon examined the wakizashi.

I nodded, outfitting the knife to my belt.

"Samurai killed themselves by cutting open their stomachs, so their guts would fall out. Huge part of the samurai honor code," Brandon said.

Everyone besides me kind of looked at him in shock, but that was Brandon, always randomly dropping obscure knowledge about everything, especially Japanese swords.

"Then, I think you've found your weapon," Sarah said.

Securing it to the left side of his belt, Brandon said,

"When I get my katana back from that bitch Marty, I'm gonna samurai fuck shit up."

We finished by choosing handguns and loading them with bullets, and then Sarah took us over to another area of the store to be outfitted with combat gear. She gestured to piles of military fatigues organized by size, so that's where we started.

Once dressed, we moved to the next shelf, which looked to be stacked with a collection of military grade composite-toe boots in tan or black. Brandon and I grabbed black boots in our sizes, and everyone else picked up tan boots.

As Sarah handed us tactical vests, she said they were also military grade like the boots, which meant they were lined not only with protection but also chock full of pockets for anything including extra ammo, matches, and gunpowder, all of which they had here.

I had to hand it to Alice. She was a definite pro with a serious supply of damn near everything. This rescue was gonna be a piece of cake.

An air of confidence swirled around the room. I knew we'd get our people back. The same feeling seemed to be written on everyone else's face, too.

We regrouped back at the table, nodding to Alice. She told us she'd been in gear from the early morning, more than ready to get her ladies away from Marty.

She laid out a plan of attack, showing us a diagram of the hospital marked with the exits that they assumed would be guarded by the fewest number of men. The main glass doors were off limits, as Alice and Carson guessed that those would be the most heavily guarded. To get in we needed to rely on fire escapes or exits and the back door.

She handed a lock picking kit to each buddy pair and showed us how to use it. I figured Brandon didn't need these instructions, but he didn't say anything. After the briefing, we had a short break. And once that was done, we'd head off in our teams in three separate vehicles.

I followed Brandon outside because he wanted to smoke, and after taking a deep inhale, he said the name of something that I didn't recognize.

"What the fuck is that?" I asked.

"Triple blend aged Irish whiskey," he said.

"They have that here?"

"Yup," he said.

"Then you owe me a drink after this is over. I'll hold you to it."

"I'll hold you, period," he said. "But yes, we'll make that happen."

"The holding?" I asked, feeling my cheeks burn.

"Super close."

Despite all our gear, and the late morning sun trying to keep us a little warm, I shivered. Brandon wrapped his arm around me, pulling me close to his body while continuing to smoke over my head.

I couldn't enjoy the moment long because Alice came out followed by Carson, Jordan, Franklin, Sarah, and Naomi.

"We're on the move, Natalie, Brandon, let's go."

Alice tossed me a set of car keys, pointing toward the car I'd be taking, a small, black two-door sports car.

Dope.

Twirling the keyring in my fingers, I looked at Brandon. "No smoking in the car."

Without acknowledging what I'd said, he dropped what little remained of his cigarette on the ground and rubbed it out with his boot.

The other buddy pairs climbed into their respective vehicles. Alice and Carson were in a jeep at the head of the convoy, and despite being in a sports car, Brandon and I were at the rear.

The drive there was quiet. Because the warehouse store was on the outskirts of town, we saw very few dead-nots driving back into the city. Only one or two staggered around.

Near the side of the road, I saw an obscenely skinny one drop after its knees buckled. No one knew exactly how dead-nots worked. Basically, they never died. Unless they got stabbed or shot in the brain, they could live forever, but their bodies continued to break down or decompose.

Feeding somehow slowed that decay, but without the energy source from human flesh, they got weaker, their bodies deteriorated faster, and they eventually dropped, unable to carry their own weight on their spindly legs.

Of course, all this was based on our observations. No one had actually studied them. So we never knew if it was the virus or something else that kept them dead-not-dead.

Sometimes we had to be careful traipsing around fields or wooded areas because ones that looked dead might just be sidelined. A bite from an incapacitated one would still be deadly.

On streets or sidewalks, the subtle head movements of an immobilized dead-not could be easily spotted. But in areas with dense cover like a heavy brush or a forest, we needed to be extra cautious.

Not much time had passed, and we came upon the hospital, a sterile white building with ten stories climbing high into the sky. Alice pulled the jeep into a parking lot shadowed behind another building about a block from the hospital. We followed and got out of the vehicles.

"I forgot to mention," Alice said. "Watch out for the runners and jumpers."

"The what?" I asked.

"We think the virus has mutated. About a month ago, we started seeing changes. A lot of them still shuffle and drag, but we've come across a few newly turned ones who can jump really high and others who run quite fast."

"Well, that's fucking terrifying," I said.

"We haven't seen any of those." Carson checked his weapons.

"We don't think there are many yet, but we've seen some. We also think the mutations start out in certain areas before they spread." Alice started unloading her gear.

"Got it. Keep an eye out, everyone." Carson said.

FOURTEEN

THE GOAL of the mission was simple: rescue the women and Steve and Akira if they were there. We had no plan to take any prisoners, nor did we want any of Marty's men to walk out of there alive. Every one of them, Marty included, existed as an obstacle to overcome. How we rid ourselves of those obstacles was entirely up to us.

We lined up flush alongside the building in front of where we'd parked. Carson went ahead of us, so he could survey the area. He looked around and then signaled at us to return to our position behind the building where the cars were parked.

"They have a guy up there, maybe on the sixth floor, with a sniper rifle," he said.

"Shit," I said.

"Don't worry," said Carson. "I'd put money on him not being a trained sniper. Regardless, we can't just walk in there. Any ideas?"

No one said a word.

After some time Brandon spoke up, "I don't suppose anyone's got any fire arrows?"

"Actually . . . ," Alice began.

"You've got to be fucking kidding me," I said.

Alice walked to the back of the jeep and tossed over a heavy canvas blanket, revealing five arrows and a bow to match. "These were in the museum. I didn't know if they'd be useful at the time, but I never say no to a weapon."

"Wow," Franklin said, eyeing the arrows.

"Forget what you may have seen in movies," Brandon explained, "because a flaming arrow likely won't stay lit while it flies through the air. The wind would knock it out of commission. So you need to soak a cloth in oil, tar, some shit like that for it to be super effective. In the absence of that, you could fill a cloth with gunpowder, and when the flames went out, the heat would be enough to cause a fire wherever the arrow landed. You got gunpowder."

"Of course we do." Alice said, even though Brandon was making a statement not asking a question.

"Okay," Carson said. "So who's going to shoot these?"

Franklin raised his hand. "I took archery lessons for five years."

"Seriously?" Sarah asked.

Franklin gave her a look that said, "Bitch, please."

I smiled, never once doubting him. Franklin had always been our very own Renaissance man.

"I guess that settles that," Alice said.

We had a simple plan. Franklin wouldn't fire directly on the sniper. Not that we could anyway. Instead, he would shoot the flaming arrows into five locations, hoping to ignite fires which would serve as misdirection so we could infiltrate the hospital.

Sarah and Jordan shredded a thick t-shirt with their edge weapons to make five pieces large enough to fill with gunpowder and tie to the arrowheads. Carson siphoned some gasoline out of the sedan Jordan had driven because it had the best gas mileage and wouldn't miss a bit of fuel. We doused the shirt in gasoline around the edges and tried to air dry them as much as possible because wet gunpowder wouldn't do shit.

When they were mostly dry, Alice filled the centers with gunpowder. Then the guys secured each piece as close to the tip of the arrowhead as tight as they could. Upon completion, we had five arrows ready to ignite.

Brandon told us an experienced sniper would move around, so we banked on this guy being inexperienced. But shooting on us from higher ground, the sniper would have the initial advantage. If he remained immobile, we'd have the ultimate advantage in the end.

Using Ruger Mark III pistols, Jordan and Sarah would fire on the sniper from different locations, as their guns had the longest range of any other weapons we had. Even though the pistols couldn't compete with a sniper rifle, they could still provide good cover fire.

Ground cover established, the rest of us, Carson, Alice, Brandon, and I, would breach the hospital. Naomi would stay on the ground with Franklin until he was finished launching the arrows, and then they'd guard the exit. It was a foolproof plan. What could go wrong?

We determined the five sites easiest to set on fire were an old overturned car with a busted out front window exposing the upholstery, a stack of cardboard boxes near a dumpster, inside the dumpster, some felled trees amid dry brush, and a laundry cart that had rolled in front of the hospital. Even if it wasn't full of laundry, the basket of the cart, made of some woven material, would surely burn.

Franklin shot the first arrow already ablaze into the car, and as expected, the flame extinguished mid-flight. But it hit the ripped upholstery, where the stuffing had fallen out. The arrow itself didn't stick into the car seat, as the point wasn't sharp enough, and the seat material was too tough.

I held my breath as we all watched. The cloth around the arrow quickly reignited, and via the gunpowder, a fire started. The first fire had the intended effect, causing the idiot sniper to fire on the car.

This minor distraction allowed Carson and Alice to move from our building to behind a large SUV in the hospital parking lot. The sniper refocused and fired on the SUV, though he didn't appear to be a pro. Carson and Alice hovered safely behind it.

The second arrow sailed through the sky and

landed short of the laundry cart but skidded, and the cloth attached to the arrow caught fire. The flames danced a little bit, climbing higher until the fabric on the side of the laundry cart caught fire.

This time, however, the sniper didn't turn toward the cart to fire, but kept on firing on Carson and Alice's position. It didn't matter because, following that, Franklin shot another arrow into the stack of boxes and then into the dumpster next to them.

Whatever had been thrown in there caught quickly, smoke billowing into the air. The literal dumpster fire distracted the sniper, allowing Carson and Alice to make it to the side exit and Brandon and me to take cover behind the SUV.

Since Carson and Alice were out of the sniper's line of sight, he turned his fire back to the SUV. Franklin had exactly one arrow remaining, one last chance to get us to the building.

Jordan and Sarah continued firing on the sniper, but he wasn't well enough exposed for them to hit him. They shattered some windows, which also helped serve as a diversion. We saw the last arrow sail into the brush, and as it did, Jordan and Sarah opened heavy fire onto the sniper's position. Brandon and I took the opening, running to the side of the building.

Alice had already picked the lock of the side door and opened it, staying out of the door frame in case someone had been on the other side, waiting to put a bullet in her chest. We heard the sniper stop firing, and Jordan and Sarah finally joined us at the door.

Seeing no one, Carson walked inside first, and we followed him, guns drawn. We decided to take it floor by floor, splitting by buddy groups. Marty probably wouldn't be using the first floor due to its exposure.

Carson and Alice would take the tenth and ninth floors, Brandon and I: eight and seven, and Jordan and Sarah would take five and four, obviously skipping the sixth floor where the sniper had been, even though he'd probably relocated by now. Better safe than sorry.

So we split up, each pair branching off on our respective floors. First Jordan and Sarah left us at five, and then Brandon and I flanked the door that led into the eighth floor, nodding to Carson and Alice as they left us.

Brandon stood on the side where the door opened with me on the other side. We quickly agreed that he would fling open the door and drop back out of sight, and I'd catch the door, holding it open. When we did, nothing happened.

Peeking through the door, we could see no one in the immediate area, and upon further exploration, we found the entire eighth floor empty. We checked every closed door and every corner. There was no one anywhere.

On the seventh floor, things went a little differently. As soon as Brandon flung open the door, shots flew through the doorway.

"How many?" I mouthed.

Brandon peered into the room and then held up

two fingers. I stood with my back pressed against the door, holding it open. I glanced at Brandon again with a look on my face that I hoped said, "what the fuck do we do?"

"We need to lure them as close to us as possible, so we can set off this." He produced a flashbang grenade.

"Shit," I whispered. "Where did you get that?"

"With the ammo and shit, duh," he said, smiling. "We fire one or two warning shots into the room. Don't wanna waste ammo. That should get those fuckers moving toward us. Ready Nat?"

I nodded. He fired one shot into the room and then motioned for me to wait. When I looked into the room, I saw two guys moving Chloe and two other women behind a nurse's station. I heaved a sigh of relief. We'd found them.

The men barked at them to get down, and they disappeared out of sight. This worked out better than I'd hoped. Even though the nurse's station consisted of a half wall, it would still protect the ladies from the flashbang. I prayed the wall would also block out some of the noise because it was about to get real loud.

When the men moved toward us, Brandon nodded at me, and I fired my one shot at them. As suspected, they dodged the bullet but continued advancing toward the door. Deeming them close enough, Brandon pulled the pin and tossed the grenade inside the room, and I let go of the door.

It closed as the flash of light and sound exploded

in their general area. The rest of the plan was pretty simple. Gut punch them with our sharp objects, letting them bleed out or die of sepsis, whichever came first. I couldn't think of better justice for rapists.

Before we opened the door and went in slicing, Brandon pulled me close to him, kissing me fast and hard.

The flashbang grenade had the intended effect. Both of the fuckheads moved around disoriented and dazed like a couple of drunks. They shouted at each other, indicating their ears were ringing.

Brandon went for one of the assholes, and I went for the other. We knocked them off balance, super easy because as Brandon explained "noise from a flashbang messes with a person's inner ear fluid, which regulates balance." Both of these big dudes went down like demolished buildings.

When the guy I'd plowed into hit the ground, I shoved my Bowie knife right into his stomach, twisting it as much as I could. Blood bubbled up and pooled out of the wound when I pulled it out. He wailed in anguish, and I couldn't resist the urge to plunge my knife in once more super close to his dick. I didn't have the stomach to cut anyone's dick off. I saw Brandon had done the same, minus the dick part, literally.

"Chloe!" I called out to her.

Chloe's head popped into view, and she roused the other two women. Her face flushed with relief, and she whipped around the nurse's station, running to me. Standing in front of the two men bleeding from their stomachs, she embraced me hard. Beyond that hug, there was no time for further pleasantries, and we all got out of there as fast as we could.

When Brandon and I got downstairs with the women, everyone else was already there, and I mean everyone. Jordan and Sarah had come back empty-handed, but they said not without killing a couple guys. Franklin and Naomi had continued firing on dead-nots from their position by the exit, saying they put down a couple of runners.

Carson and Alice had beaten us downstairs and had Steve and Akira with them. Steve reported that the backpack he carried was practically bursting with formula. Akira looked bigger than when I'd seen him last, definitely looking like a more well-fed baby. Amazing what a few days of food will do for a kid.

Upon exiting the hospital, Chloe went straight for Carson, and he put his arms around her and didn't let go for what seemed like an eternity.

"We've got to move and now!" The urgency in Alice's voice broke up their tender moment.

Dead-nots seemed to come from nowhere as we cut a path back to the vehicles. Chloe said she wanted to be with Carson, and he held tight to her hand the whole way to the jeep. They climbed into the back, and one of the other girls joined Alice in the front.

Before the rest of us could get into the other cars, we heard a hoarse voice scream the word "wait." Marty. She clutched her chest, dragging herself toward us. Her clothes were soaked crimson. She had a gun in her hand, and while not pointed at any one person in particular, she aimed toward our group.

The noise she made caught the attention of the surrounding dead-nots, and they dragged themselves closer. My eyes darted around, assessing the threat, and I hoped none of them were runners.

Though Alice spoke to Carson, she turned to Marty, eyes wide. "I shot her. I thought she was dead."

Carson and Alice got out of the jeep, but I noticed Chloe and the other woman stayed in the vehicle.

"The girl . . . " Marty's words came out amid gasps.

Because we'd rescued three women, Chloe and two of Alice's chicks, confusion spread across our faces. Not that it mattered. Marty had no right to demand anything from any of the women.

I looked at Chloe, and her face was fearful. Alice's friend, the one in the passenger seat, reached over and grabbed Chloe's hand. Marty stumbled, righted herself, and then continued to advance on us.

"Stop moving." Carson walked toward Marty.

The rest of us picked off some dead-nots that had straggled close to us. An eerie calm settled in, and it got super quiet until we could no longer see or hear anything but Marty. I don't know why she'd bothered to chase after us. Marty'd been shot; she was as good as zombified.

"You should know . . . ," Marty started, her voice quiet, breathy. "Your girl . . . your Chloe . . . "

"You're finished, Marty. To be honest, I don't care

what you have to say." Carson turned his back on her and walked to the jeep.

I looked at Chloe, who curled her hands around her stomach as if trying to protect something precious.

FIFTEEN

NO ONE MOVED EXCEPT CHLOE, who now clutched her midsection.

"It's true," Chloe said, her voice almost a whisper. "I've known for a while now. It wasn't one of Marty's disgusting men, though."

The gravity of what she'd said settled on us one by one. She lifted her gaze from her belly and looked directly at Carson.

"It's yours," she said to him.

Everything made sense to me now. Why Chloe had seemed disinterested in me. Why she'd spent so much time sleeping. Why she'd remained close to Carson at every opportunity.

I looked from Chloe to Carson. His eyes had grown watery, and he moved away from Marty and toward Chloe in the jeep.

We still all had guns drawn on Marty, who'd crumpled to the ground. She looked like less of a threat than the dead-nots still shuffling our way. So we pulled focus from her and fired on them.

But I wanted to see Carson and Chloe and turned my attention back to them. He stood next to her outside the jeep, clasping her hands in his.

"Our baby," he said, smiling.

I'd never seen Carson this happy. Ever. But if it were me, I would have thought twice about bringing a kid into this nightmare of a world.

Chloe nodded at Carson, and he cupped her face into his hand and kissed her tenderly. When she cried, her tears looked like ones of joy rather than sadness.

"I wanted to tell you, but I wanted to be sure first," Chloe said. "Marty tested me while we were still at the police station, and then she tested me again at the hospital. Definitely pregnant."

"I . . . I always wanted kids," Carson said, keeping his voice low. "I mean before everything."

"I remember you telling me that," she said. "I wish it had happened under better circumstances, baby."

"Me too," he said, pressing his forehead to hers.

"I hate to break up such a beautiful moment of tenderness, but I think we should get out of here," Alice said.

Carson snapped out of his moment with Chloe. "Right."

Alice and Carson climbed back into the jeep.

"What about her?" Hovering, Brandon motioned to Marty still on the ground, gasping for breath like a fish out of water.

"It's funny," said Carson. "I suddenly don't care what happens to her."

On her knees, Marty clawed at her chest while still trying to suck in air. Marty had been a problem, sure, but she hadn't been *my* biggest problem. If the people she'd wronged the most wanted to leave her here, then so be it. I moved to get in the car.

"Carson . . . wait . . . you, you can't leave me," Marty begged.

"Looks like you have a gun." Carson's words were icy.

"And one bullet," Marty said, understanding what she was meant to do with it.

Carson would not be merciful today. Preventing Marty from walking through this world as a dead-not was the kindest thing anyone could do for her, but neither Carson nor any of us felt she deserved even a modicum of kindness. Not after what she'd done to Alice and to us.

After taking out some more approaching dead-nots, Brandon shrugged and got in the car. Jordan and Franklin walked to the jeep so Franklin could hug Chloe. Then Alice's other woman, Naomi, Sarah, and Steve plus the attached Akira were the last ones to move toward the cars.

After brief hugs and squeals of joy from Franklin, he rejoined Jordan's side. I climbed into the driver's seat of the sports car.

Marty dragged herself to the building next to where we'd parked and propped herself up against the brick wall. "Please . . . Carson . . . "

Carson didn't say anything else, and Alice started up the jeep and pulled into the road. But the others were still negotiating some things. Jordan said he wanted Sarah to take Naomi and the other unnamed girl in the car she'd driven here. He said he wouldn't mind taking Steve and the baby. This negotiation seemed to take longer than necessary, and I kept an eye on the horizon, making sure dead-nots didn't approach them.

Windows down, I idled behind Alice, continuing to watch them from my review mirror discuss who would go where. I lowered the convertible top, and Brandon popped up, taking out a few dead-nots who had staggered near.

"Come on. Hurry," I grumbled.

Jordan had the keys to one car in his hand, and Sarah had the keys to the other, and it looked like they'd finally decided on the travel arrangements when I heard a gunshot shatter the silence. No one seemed to move for an eternity.

When I finally gathered the courage to turn my head, the first place I looked was Marty. It felt as if slow motion had sped up. I saw her drop the gun to her lap, and my eyes went everywhere, looking for what she'd done.

Jordan's cries ripped through the air as he ran to the passenger side where Franklin had fallen. I got out of the car and ran to where he'd propped Franklin up against the door.

I immediately leaned Franklin forward and tried

to put pressure on his back where Marty had shot him. Tears streamed down Jordan's face.

The sounds of the women and Steve crying out and crowding around Jordan and Franklin drowned out everything else. Tears stung my eyes, and I couldn't stop them from falling.

Standing up, his face twisted in agony, Jordan barreled toward Marty. The corners of her mouth turned up in a smile, and Jordan screamed as he unloaded several bullets into her chest. Satisfied that she was finally dead, he waited a few beats and then put a bullet in her skull.

Gasping for breath like he'd sprinted from two blocks away, Franklin's entire face twisted in pain. I feared the worst when he coughed up blood. The bullet had likely punctured one of his lungs. I could think of very few scenarios in this world where he would survive a gunshot wound, punctured lung or not.

"Jordan . . . " Franklin gasped for breath.

"It's not necessary to talk," Jordan said.

"Well . . . that's . . . fucking ridiculous," Franklin said.

No one else said anything, and aside from me trying to stop the bleeding, everyone backed away, giving Jordan and Franklin their space. No one could do anything. While Jordan's tears stained his face, Franklin smiled through his.

"Jordy . . . I've never . . . loved anyone . . . the way I love you," he said.

"We are of same mind." Jordan said, his voice so quiet now.

"You always . . . made me feel like . . . this world . . . wasn't such a bad world," Franklin said. "And that . . . if I had to be . . . stuck here . . . I'm glad I was . . . stuck here . . . with you."

The pauses between his words got longer, and Jordan's tears fell harder. He held tight to Franklin's hand and pushed his face close, kissing his lips and then both his cheeks.

"If I had to . . . do it all . . . over . . . again . . . I wouldn't . . . change a thing." Franklin rested his forehead on Jordan's cheek. "I love you . . . more than . . . coffee."

That made Jordan cough out a small laugh, but his face soon clouded with devastation. "Please do not leave me. I need you."

"You've never . . . needed anyone." Franklin's head rolled to the side slightly.

"That alone should speak volumes because I most definitely need you," Jordan said, cupping his hand around Franklin's head.

Franklin reached for Jordan's other hand and wrapped his fingers around it using as much strength as he could. Silent tears ran down my face.

"You'll be . . . fine," Franklin said. "I love you."

"I love you too, so much." Jordan choked out the words.

Franklin's eyes fluttered closed and his breathing stopped. Jordan collapsed on top of his body and wept.

My knees felt like they could no longer support my weight, so I scooted back and sat away from Jordan. He didn't need me in his space right now. Attempting to wipe away my tears with my arm did no good. They just kept coming.

The air was thick with sadness. Chloe had tear-stained cheeks, and even Steve wiped his face.

Jordan stayed locked onto Franklin, his body moving up and down in sobs.

After several moments, Carson moved close to Jordan and put his hand on his shoulder. It was time. Jordan had to get up, and Franklin had to die again.

I tried to wipe some of the blood off my hands on the back of my pants, but it was still there, staining my fingers. Blood stays. It always stays.

I struggled to get Jordan to his feet, pulling him until he relented his grip on Franklin. He crashed into me. So I did the only thing I could do at that moment. I wrapped my arms around him as he continued sobbing.

I'd always hoped to find a love like theirs. To me, they'd always been a model of a happy, loving couple.

I moved Jordan, making sure his face was turned away from Franklin's body. Carson seemed to wrestle with the best way to do it, though I knew he didn't want to do it all. None of us would have wanted that job.

I squeezed my eyes shut as the shot rang out. I could feel Jordan's body jerk at the sound.

His sobs intensified, and I tightened my grip on him.

SIXTEEN

INSIDE THE SAFETY of the warehouse store, everyone kinda went their separate ways. No one spoke. What was there to say anyway?

Holding my hand, Brandon walked me over to the large table and sat me down. He climbed over the chair in front of me before sitting down.

Hadn't we discussed the last pieces of this rescue only moments ago? No, that had happened this morning. When I noticed Franklin's mint green coffee cup, still on the table, I teared up again.

Brandon didn't say anything, and I appreciated his moments of silence now more than ever. Instead, he opened up a bottle of clear alcohol and poured a little bit on some baby wipes he'd pulled from a package. He wiped the dried blood from my hands and arms with a sort of tenderness a parent shows their injured child. My eyes focused on him, but I didn't see anything. Not really. I felt numb.

In between wipes he took swigs from the bottle

and so did I, trying to numb myself inside too. I looked around for Jordan, but I didn't see him anywhere. Despite this place being mostly big and open, it still had lots of little nooks to disappear into.

When I looked around a second time, I saw that Chloe had gone over to where the children were playing, Carson following close behind. This place had tons of stuff for kids: toys and books, shit like that. I guess she thought she might want to learn how to get along with children, as she was bound to be a mother soon enough.

Steve was also in the kid's area, and the children were giddy at the sight of Akira and his mop of black hair. They poked and tickled him, trying to make him smile and laugh.

When Steve passed the baby, to Chloe, she seemed a bit apprehensive at first, but then quickly acclimated to holding the child. It looked like motherhood was a role she'd been made for.

The happiness that existed there proved a stark contrast to the mood we'd brought back with us. I kinda wished I was a kid then, innocent to tragedy.

Our group was now colored in both happiness and sadness at the same time. How was that even possible? I guess we were all on this rollercoaster of joy and pain together.

I felt stuck, idling in heartbreak. The world seemed a little darker and a little colder without Franklin in it.

Guilt hit me hard, like I hadn't cherished my time with Franklin more, and I felt even worse that I knew so little about Jordan. Franklin had been Jordan's everything, and without him Jordan might be completely alone. Even though we didn't always see eye to eye, no one deserved to be on their own in this world.

How could I fix this? I was helpless. Unable to bring Franklin back, I clearly couldn't unfuck the past. Breathing out a heavy sigh, my body ached with exhaustion. I had no answers.

Brandon finished cleaning me off and dragged me to our fort. He moved aside the blanket door, and I crawled in. He followed me.

He leaned back on the cushions and held his arms out to me. "Let me hold you."

Without speaking, I collapsed down into his arms, and he folded them around me. For someone who often felt like she didn't fit anywhere, I fit here, in Brandon's grip. For the first time all day, an overwhelming sense of peace rushed over me. But my head was still in a bad way.

"I think she wanted to die," I blurted out. "Marty. I think she *really* wanted to die."

"She definitely wanted to die," Brandon said.

"I should've done more."

"What else could you have done?" It had meant to be rhetorical because his tone indicated, *You did all you could, Natalie.*

But I answered him anyway. "I could've killed Marty. I could've killed her when she tried to get Carson to end her life."

"No way any of us could have guessed that she was gonna do what she did," he said.

No other words could express the feeling tearing my insides apart, but Brandon answered my silence by tightening his hold on me.

I don't remember much of what happened after that. Heavy with weight of everything this day had done to us pushed me into sleep.

In the morning, I had no desire to extract myself from our blanket fort nor from the comfort of Brandon's arms. However, fierce cold and unbelievable hunger assaulted me.

I couldn't remember the last time I'd eaten. I often thought that Brandon could survive on very little food, and if I never said anything about eating, he probably wouldn't either.

"Hey." I nudged him. "Let's go eat something."

He murmured agreement, and we climbed out of the blanket fort. I had no idea what time it was, but people were mulling around doing different things.

Chloe and Carson rocked back and forth on a porch swing. She gave me a wave and a half smile when Brandon and I walked by. Serious-face Carson gave a cursory nod.

The children played, carrying around Baby Akira like he was a chunky doll. They poked his chubby cheeks and erupted in giggles.

Alice and Sarah sat at the big table, holding hands and sipping on mugs of coffee. The rich smell wafted through the immediate area, and I frowned as my thoughts landed on Franklin.

"Mom!" Hazel said, running over.

"Yeah honey?" Sarah said.

"Bobby and I made this for you!" Hazel handed Sarah a bright paper flower.

"It's beautiful!" Sarah said.

"Don't worry Mama," Hazel said. "We're makin' one for you next!"

"I'm not at all worried, sweetheart" Alice said to her and then turned to me. "You two hungry?"

"Definitely," I said.

She dipped a ladle into a pot sitting on a propane stove, and handed me a bowl full of thick amber-colored stuff and then passed one to Brandon. The spiciness curled into my nose.

"Hazel and Bobby were both conceived via IVF back when the world was still the world and technology was at an all-time high," Alice said.

"Since I carried the babies in my womb, I'm Mom," Sarah said.

"And I'm Mama," Alice said. "It turned out that I was infertile, not that I ever told Marty that. I needed her to believe Hazel was my own child, so I could use that leverage to escape. Anyway, I couldn't donate my eggs to be implanted into Sarah. However, my brother kindly donated sperm for us, so in a way the children are both biologically ours. Not that it matters now, but I adopted them as soon as they were born, so they're legally ours as well. Even though that world doesn't exist anymore, it was important to me that we made certain the children would always be our family in all ways."

While Alice and Sarah told us about their family, the noise of the children echoed throughout the warehouse, but besides their playful sounds, everything else was still, quiet. It was a bright spot in a string of bad days to hear about how two people so in love could create their own family together and live through all this despite how awful the world was. Alice and Sarah twined their fingers together.

As I looked around, I could see everyone except for Jordan, and I wondered if he was okay. I couldn't imagine how he felt, getting his heart ripped out like that.

Had Brandon been killed right in front of me, I probably would have behaved the same way, inconsolable, holed up somewhere.

Things had settled down in this world. Our people had been rescued, and since we had a reasonable handle on battling the dead-nots, we were in no imminent danger from anything.

So how does one kill time in the midst of a dead-not apocalypse? We'd spent so much time constantly tense. Did any of us even know how to relax anymore? The behaviors of everyone I'd observed today answered my question for me. They certainly did.

After stuffing our faces, Brandon and I meandered back to the blanket fort. Neither one of us felt like doing much of anything else anyway. Thinking seriously about it, we were all probably way beyond tired. Things had been nonstop for who knows how long.

It made me feel somewhat happy to spend a day wrapped in blankets and Brandon's arms, drowning in books. We'd stopped at the book table before we hid ourselves away for the day.

Inside our nook Brandon clicked the switch of the twinkle lights, and because I was sufficiently warmed by the curry, I took off my hoodie, revealing a low cut tank top. I hadn't meant to be sexy, but that was apparently the effect. Brandon's eyes boring into me served as a much needed distraction.

"Meow."

"I have a question," I said.

"Wait," he said. "I'm still gazing."

I wanted so badly to touch him, so I reached out and lightly dragged my fingers across the tattoo on his arm.

"How am I supposed to concentrate on questions?" He closed his eyes, breathing out an almost inaudible sigh.

"They're fun questions though," I said. "Unless you'd rather talk about sex."

"I was staring at your boobs so duh. But no, ask me."

I didn't take my hand off his arm. "You have the opportunity to do whatever you want, be as reckless as you want, so what do you do?"

He didn't answer my question. "Do you really wanna have sex with me again?"

"I would not hesitate. Is that you being reckless? Fucking me?"

"For me, it would be nice, not reckless. That's

what other people would say. 'Oh, he was so reckless.' Nope, I was home."

My face felt like it was on fire. How did he always manage to do that? He always made me forget that anyone or anything existed in this world. I tackled him in an embrace, knocking him backwards into a pile of blankets and pillows.

"Nat—"

"Shut up, Brandon. Just kiss me."

We couldn't get out of our clothes fast enough. It was sloppy, not like those romance movies, where the removal of each piece of clothing matched the beat of some sexy music. No, not like that at all. It didn't matter though. I wasn't a character in a movie.

When I felt his bare skin next to mine for the first time in years, I couldn't stop the tears from falling. I couldn't go any farther than this, and my whole body trembled.

What the actual fuck was wrong with me? I'd wanted this for years, dreamed about it, fantasized about it, and now the only thing I could do was nothing.

Without warning, Brandon shoved me off of him, not roughly, but I got the message. He didn't want me touching him anymore right now.

I wanted him, my body wanted him, and I know he felt the same. I could see it. But I froze, unable to move in the direction we'd both wanted.

He slipped on his pants, didn't bother with a shirt, grabbed his cigarettes, and pulled back the blanket to let himself out.

I balled up my hoodie between my fists, my tears dripping onto the fabric. I couldn't do anything but watch the gentle movement of the blanket door as it stilled after he left.

Only when I was certain that he'd put a considerable distance between us, I collapsed into the pillow and sobbed.

SEVENTEEN

TEETERING on the precipice between sleep and awake, I felt Brandon's body nuzzle in next to me until his lips were near my ear. "Sorry."

His warmth swallowed me as the ashen, chemical stench of a lifetime of stubbed out cigarettes burnt my nostrils. I wrinkled my nose. It didn't matter how often I'd been around Brandon smoking, I'd never get used to it.

Just like I'd never get used to his reckless abandonment. I tried to wiggle away from him, but he pulled me tighter, trying to bury his face in my neck. I felt like I couldn't breathe.

I flipped around, attempting to sear his skin with a look. "Well, you fucked off at the absolute worst time."

"I had to step away 'cause it was all emotionally." Even the adorable way Brandon said things wasn't enough to win me over this time.

"Now you know what I feel like. All. The. Time.

You make me feel a special kind of stupid lust that I can't do anything about." I lowered my voice. "I wish I could fucking stop feeling that way, but I want you near me. I can't help it."

"Ok, you can't start getting me all squishy again." He pulled my body toward his again, and I didn't roll away this time. "I told you. Being with you, it feels like home."

"I didn't think anything would ever feel like home again. But you're right. No one knows the nerd me like you do. No one ever has."

"Nerdy girls were always my Achilles," he said, lips curing in a smile.

I could feel the heat stinging my cheeks, and I almost covered my face for fear of looking ridiculous, gushing over Brandon like a teenager with a crush.

Attempting to distract myself, I picked up the book and flipped to the page where we'd left off. "How about the reads?"

"You know I'm all about the reads. Just like I'm all about you," he said.

"Shut up," I said.

Dumb Brandon. Always making my insides feel like jelly. He knew it too, so I suppose that made him Smart Brandon. The look on his face, his ear-to-ear grin screamed he knew all my secrets. It was infuriating and alluring at the same time. The enigma of Brandon.

I tried to ignore my super strong desire to kiss him, paging through the book to find where we'd left off.

We talked a little more, and then I read as the day dragged on into night, driving us to sleep.

Days passed like this. Brandon and I just chilling in our blanket fort, reading books and getting all snuggly. We only emerged for bathroom breaks or to eat. We hardly spent any time with anyone else.

"Hey, Nat, wake up." Brandon kept poking me until I opened my eyes.

I felt shrouded in a haze, trying to rub the sleep away. I looked up at him, a question in my eyes.

"Wanna blow some shit up?"

"Oh." I thought I must be dreaming, and dream Nat had only one answer. "Hell yes."

It turned out I had not dreamt it. With the sling of an automatic weapon draped over his shoulder, Brandon dragged me out of the blanket fort and showed me my red wagon. It contained several cans of spray paint, a fire extinguisher, one large propane tank, and a number of smaller propane tanks, some ammo, as well as flares.

Brandon giggled.

"What are you giggling about?" I asked, but I couldn't help but smile.

From his hand, the one that had been behind his back, he produced a grenade. "I found this."

"Seriously? A fucking grenade!"

"Not just any grenade, Nat. This is an M67 also known as a baseball grenade because, duh, it's shaped like a ball and thus can be thrown like one, too. A good arm can chuck one up to a hundred feet, and once the pin is removed, it'll 'splode in about five seconds."

Brandon's excitement infected me. I never tired of hearing him talk about things he loved, and he loved weapons.

"I've never blown anything up before." I grinned up at him, already feeling the rush of adrenaline at the thrill.

"Follow my lead, grasshopper." He returned my smile, which felt like bathing in warm sunshine.

He threw a blanket over the contents of the wagon and pulled it to the back door. The thick brick exterior made this place much different from when we'd camped out in houses. Most times, like now, no one needed to be on guard duty, so we slipped out the back door undetected.

When Brandon opened the door, we were swallowed by darkness. Neither one of us had spoken to the group about leaving camp. Of all the people we had to worry about, a pissed off Carson would be the worst of them. Even though I didn't know the others all that well, I knew an angry Carson would suck to deal with. But right now, I didn't care.

I held the door while Brandon grabbed a roll of duct tape he wore like a bracelet, pulling it off his wrist. He taped both sides of the latch so that we wouldn't be locked out but could still close the door.

He pulled the wagon through the parking lot until we reached the end of the concrete. From there, a stretch of flat open land sprawled out before us. I couldn't see a single tree and only sparse sections of grasses and shrubbery. An abandoned car with busted out windows sat a short distance from the end of the parking lot.

"Perfect." He looked the car up and down, as if the gears in his head were spinning up a plan. "That'll give us some height."

We bent over the wagon, examining its contents together like looking into a baby crib.

"What should we blow up first?" he asked.

"The propane tanks?" I asked.

He grabbed two small tanks, and I took the other two. We jogged to the car and set the four tanks in a row lengthwise on top of it. Then he ignited two flares and put them in between the first and second and the third and fourth tanks. After that, we walked a short distance away from the car somewhere around a hundred yards, give or take.

Always the gentleman, Brandon let me shoot first. Under normal circumstances, I was a pretty decent shot. However, I thought the darkness might make me a crap shot, and I wouldn't be able to hit one of the tanks. Funny, I decided to blame the darkness when the truth was that I didn't have much experience with an automatic rifle. Handgun, fine. Bowie knife, without a doubt. But it's not like automatic weapons were just sitting around a dead-not apocalypse. This wasn't a video game.

Brandon pointed out the purpose of the flares, illuminating a little of the surrounding area. "So you don't fuck up your shots, Nat."

Whether or not he could see it, I narrowed my brow. "Hey, I'm not a bad shot."

"If you say so," he said.

The flares fizzed in the darkness, casting enough light to aim at the tanks using the scope of the rifle. Brandon loaded the rounds into the chamber. After he was finished, he handed it to me. I puffed out a grunt as I hoisted up the weapon. What the fuck did this thing weigh?

I could see Brandon grinning at me the whole time. I *had* to hit my target now, lest I never hear the end of it from him.

Through the scope, I eyed the leftmost propane tank, taking aim at it. I sucked in a quick breath and fired, refusing to let it out until I heard the screech of the round ripping through the tank. The swell of gas bent the air around it until it caught the flare, causing a blossom of fire to bloom into the sky.

With a smirk, I passed the rifle to Brandon. I watched him take aim, and my back prickled with sweat. Not sure if it was because I felt the heat or had gotten turned on. Probably a bit of both.

He aimed at the rightmost tank and fired. The round tore through the propane tank and as soon as the gas licked the flare, it rippled up into a fireball of Hollywood proportions, which reflected in his eyes.

I couldn't see anything else. As usual, I only saw Brandon, in a t-shirt, the muscles in his wiry arms relaxing as he passed the weapon back to me. With nothing else to focus on, the tension in my stomach seemed to dissolve, lifting the weight of the crapload of stuff that had happened recently from my shoulders.

The sun peeked over the horizon, causing the clouds in the sky to glow orange. My eyes didn't leave Brandon as he lifted the large propane tank with a low grunt and carried it to the car. I didn't know what he planned to do with it, but I bounced on my heels, eager to find out.

I dragged my eyes away from Brandon and looked around. I couldn't see anything. The area was still and quiet, free of moans or any movement whatsoever. It seemed weird.

Hadn't there always been at least one of those nasty, rotting things in our vicinity at all times? Why hadn't they ventured out here? Was the warehouse store too off the beaten path?

Yet, every time the wind blew up some dirt or trash, I thought I saw a dead-not. I shook my head. My mind always picked the worst times to play tricks on me.

Brandon jogged back to me with a sly grin on his face. "Ready?"

"Oh yes," I said, matching his smile.

He went to the wagon and pawed around it until he produced the little baseball of the M67 grenade. I went wide-eyed as he made motions of throwing the grenade. I couldn't help but feel a little giddy anticipating the biggest explosion I'd ever seen in my life.

I held my breath as he pulled the pin and chucked the grenade. I still couldn't breathe, as it bounced slightly before landing an inch past the propane tank and right in front of the car.

The sound drained from the immediate area, swallowed up by the boom of the grenade exploding. When it did, the gas consumed the flares and morphed into a fiery tulip, the force of the explosion flipping the car. The surrounding area disappeared in the plume of flame.

I ambled backward and then regained my footing. "That. Was. Awesome!"

He picked me up in a hug and spun me around, and I kissed him. When he put me down, I couldn't help but, scan the perimeter for any dead-nots. The fire crackled, its flames continuing to lick the sky, when a bit of movement caught my eye.

EIGHTEEN

TWO DEAD-NOTS SPRINTED in our direction, their blood-streaked arms flailing, cutting through the early morning air like propellers. They weren't running toward us, but to the explosion we'd caused. The flames had subsided slightly, but the fire still burned like a beacon into the sky.

I yanked up the rifle, which I'd slung around my shoulder while Brandon had been busy hocking the grenade at the car. I shot at one, but it turned its head, and the shot missed.

"Fuck," I mumbled, sliding the rifle to my back.

Hitting that propane tank earlier had really been dumb luck because I clearly had no idea how to shoot this big gun. I traded it for my handgun, but the dead-not was almost on me, so I jumped back and shot out its foot, causing it to spill forward.

I couldn't see Brandon anymore, only this fucker in front of me trying to grab my legs. I dropped to my knee on its chest, shoving my Bowie knife into its skull.

Flipping my hair out of my face, I got to my feet, and then I saw Brandon, standing off to the side with his arms crossed, smiling.

"Not one word," I said.

Still grinning, Brandon shook his head.

The door of the warehouse store flung open. Carson barreled toward us. His cheeks were puffed and red, his exposed teeth clamped together.

When Brandon turned toward him, Carson punched him right in the face. Though Brandon staggered back a couple of steps, he didn't fall.

I heard the crack of his neck as Brandon twisted his head back. Then he started wailing on Carson. All I saw was fist after fist after fist until Carson ended up on the ground. Brandon hovered over him, staring hard with a look that said, "try me and I'll give you another."

My breath quickened. I didn't know what to do, so I hovered in the background, hoping the car fire would swallow me whole.

Carson was no small guy, and I knew he wouldn't lie down and take being pummeled on. So it came as no surprise when he jumped back to his feet. As Brandon turned his head to spit, Carson punched him in the gut. Brandon went back at him, and the two devolved into a tangle of limbs.

Barely dressed, Chloe ran out, ending up on the outskirts of the fight. She screamed, while keeping her distance from the guys. I didn't want to get involved in their mess, either. When her eyes met mine, I knew we were on the same page.

She yelled at Carson to stop, like she expected him to be the one to end their fight. I didn't do anything. I should've. I just . . . didn't.

The wrestling, grunting, and punching continued until both guys' faces were blood-smeared. Even though Carson had a bigger build than Brandon, Brandon knew how to fight and fight well. I had no idea how long they'd keep at it, and not having an answer to that compelled me to finally stop them.

"Stop! Brandon, Carson stop!" I didn't touch them because I didn't want to get my face beat as well, so I continued trying to shout some sense into them. "It was my idea!"

Brandon and Carson stopped hammering on each other. One after the other, they jumped to their feet, and Brandon spit a glob of blood into the dirt.

"It was my idea to come out here and blow shit up, so if you wanna pound on someone, it should be me!" I balled my fists as if preparing to take a gut-punch.

Carson wiped some blood pouring from his nose. "Have you lost your goddamn mind, Natalie?"

"I'm sorry. I wasn't thinking." My eyes tried to find something interesting in the dirt to stare at instead of looking Carson in the eye.

He took a step closer to me. "You put all of us in danger! Chloe and the children. Those explosions were deafening. This place could have been surrounded with dead-nots!"

Wiping his face with the back of his arm, Brandon appeared at my side as, if daring Carson to move closer to me. No one else moved.

By now everyone else, except for the children, had come outside. In various states, they all stared at Brandon, Carson, and me. Alice and Sarah were there. Naomi hovered in the background, and Steve came without Akira. Every single adult we knew stood in a semicircle around us, except for Jordan.

"Natalie! Goddammit! Are you listen—"

"Carson, wait." My eyes darted around the crowd of people. "Jordan, where's Jordan?"

Everyone's eyes were fixed on Carson and me, until I asked about Jordan. They started scanning the crowd, faces muddled with confusion.

Steve shattered the discord, his voice just over a whisper. "I haven't seen him since we came back without Franklin."

"Me either." Even though Jordan hadn't been a regular social butterfly, he'd always been somewhere around, with a book or a mug of tea in hand.

"Well." Carson blew out a breath. "Let's go look for him.

The skylights of the warehouse store had let the light of the day inside. Carson told us to split up and leave no area of the place unturned. Brandon and I walked away from the group and started searching the store.

"Why did you take the fall for that?" He wiped blood off his face with his shirt.

"I dunno, Brandon. I guess I just really like your face, and I don't wanna see it beat to a bloody pulp."

He grinned down at me. "I think I was doing my share of the face beating out there."

"I'm sure Chloe is a fan of Carson's face just the same," I said. "Nothing was really being solved with said beating, and it didn't hurt me at all to take the blame. I gambled on Carson not pounding my face in."

I didn't mind lying for Brandon, especially if it pushed him closer to me. But he didn't need anyone's help, let alone mine. So why did I think I needed to help him? It looked like it had become me trying to do anything to keep him by my side. No matter how that thing might end up hurting me.

NINETEEN

MY SEARCH with Brandon produced nothing, but while we were in the midst of it, Naomi came running from the back of the store.

"Natalie!" Naomi jogged toward me with something in her hand. "We found a letter. It's got your name on it."

She produced the letter, and my name was the only thing written in beautiful calligraphy on the sealed envelope. I wrinkled my brow at Brandon. He answered with a shrug.

By now, everyone had finished searching and crowded around me. I clutched the letter, the only clue we had. I opened it. The fancy calligraphy inside matched the outside.

Dear Natalie,

I am not sure if I have the words to properly express my feelings fully. In short, my heart is shattered beyond repair. During the quiet times, Franklin often spoke of how you reminded him of his sister. You had the same dry sense of humor and mannerisms as she did. He said that your presence was comforting for him and helped him remember the better days. Even though he only knew you a short time, he always cherished the moments you two spent together, and he said he felt like he had known you his whole life. Because of this and his love for you and despite our differences, I feel like I owe you an explanation more than anyone else. I have decided to leave the group. I am aware of the fact that this place is safer than anything I could find on my own, but believe me when I say that safety and survival are no longer paramount. Franklin was my entire life. I had no life before him, and I have no life without him. I cannot imagine walking through any world without him let alone this miserable world. I have decided that I can no longer be around people or things that remind me of him. Please do not come after me. There are far greater priorities than chasing after someone who has no desire to be found. Take care of yourself and be comforted in the knowledge that Franklin loved you.

Sincerely,

Jordan

Tears burned in my eyes. I looked up from the letter to everyone still staring at me as if expecting me to say something. I swallowed hard, attempting to stop the tears from falling.

"He's gone," I whispered. "Jordan . . . he left."

"Left?" Steve asked. "As in for good? He's not coming back?"

"That's what he said." I held up the letter. "He said he can't be around anything that reminds him of Franklin anymore. And we shouldn't try to look for him because he doesn't wanna be found."

I folded the letter and put it in my pocket. I looked at Carson and then at the faces of everyone else. No one made any effort to say anything.

After a moment, Steve's voice cut through the silence. "I don't think Franklin would want us to just let him go like that."

"When did you become his best friend?" I asked, my ears burning with anger. "How about you shut the fuck up?"

Steve dropped his shoulders, eyeing his shoes.

"Carson, we gotta go after him," I said. "I wouldn't wanna be out there all alone."

"Here we go again," Brandon said, rolling his eyes.

"Only a search party," Carson said, gritting his teeth.

Nodding her agreement, Alice said she'd check on the vehicles and jogged out to the door to the back parking lot. She returned a few minutes later. "The white sedan is gone, the one he was driving when we went to rescue the women from Marty."

"Bet he's got a massive head start on us," Brandon said.

"I think we should at least try. Should be safe if we remain mobile," I said.

"I agree with Natalie. Regardless, this mission is on a volunteer basis only. I won't force anyone to go," Carson said.

"I'm in," I said. "Obviously."

Brandon threw up his hands. "Let's ride."

"You guys had our backs when we needed you, so you have our support," Alice said, gesturing to Sarah.

"That settles it," Carson said. "Natalie, Brandon, Alice, Sarah, and I will— "

"And me," Chloe said. "I'm going too."

"No goddamn way," said Carson.

Chloe's laugh was threatening. "What do you mean 'no goddamn way?' I'm not a porcelain doll, Cars."

"Chloe, you're pregnant. There is no way I would put you in harm's way," Carson said.

"Then don't," Chloe said. "I trust you, and everyone else here for that matter, to cover me."

"I don't want you going. I forbid it. End of discussion," Carson said.

I scoffed. Chloe's eyes narrowed, and Carson definitely wasn't gonna win this one.

"Excuse me? You *'forbid it? End of discussion?'* I didn't realize that I was your ward. You better believe I'm going now. If you don't want me riding with you, I'll ride with someone else," Chloe said.

Carson reached for Chloe's hands. "Chloe, you're going to be the mother of our baby. You don't *need* to go on this rescue. You need to stay here."

"I didn't realize this was the 1800s, and I'd been put on bed rest. Tell me, Dr. Carson, what else do I *need* to do?" Chloe backed away from him, folding her arms across her chest.

He looked like he was about to open his mouth to say something but snapped it shut, obviously changing his mind.

"All right, baby," he breathed out.

Carson may have been an asshole, but it looked to me like acquiescing to Chloe's desire to help sucked all the life out of him. Even though he said it in a totally dumbass way, I know he protested because he just wanted her and the baby to be safe. We all did.

Since none of us knew when Jordan left, there was no way to know how long a head-start he had on us. It also didn't help that we had no idea where he'd be headed.

We geared up, taking fewer weapons than the rescue mission, which meant one sharp plus a firearm. We didn't need automatic rifles, grenades, or fire arrows for a search. We dropped the tactile vests, opting for boots, long-sleeved shirts and jackets, denim or leather pants.

Earlier I'd been writing lost notes in my kitten notebook, and I remembered jotting down how best to prepare for dead-nots.

Gearing up for a run in with dead-nots:

1. Keep any appendages which are prone to bites, like arms and legs, well covered.

2. Long sleeves, layers, and pants and jackets with some thickness are best.

This time, Alice and Sarah would take the jeep. Brandon and I got our sleek black sports car again, and Carson and Chloe, once she stopped being mad at him for his earlier misogyny, would take the pickup truck that Alice had picked us up in when she first brought us here.

Before we set off, Brandon popped outside to smoke, while everyone else was getting the rest of their gear ready. I sat on the small trunk of the car, and he leaned back into me nestling between my legs, draping his arm on my thigh.

"It's always something," he said, exhaling.

I didn't know what to say. It did always seem like that, like we never stopped doing something or chasing after something when all I wanted to do was sit under twinkle lights and read. If I asked Brandon, he'd probably say the same.

We sat like this for a while, Brandon close to me, leaning against the car, smoking, his hand on my leg. A chill lingered in the air outside, but there was no wind. I couldn't hear anything except the sounds of Brandon puffing out smoke. No sounds from dead-nots drifted into our space.

Something about this moment reminded me of the time Brandon and I were sprawled on his bed with the sunlight streaking through down-turned blinds. His hands rested on my bare legs, not burdened by all these heavy clothes.

The heat of summer crept into the room. Brandon put on a movie, one he'd seen but I hadn't. Some independent film called *Gerry*, that I'd never even heard of but had some well-known actors in it, played on the small screen.

He insisted I watch it, but not too long after he put the movie on, he fell asleep. I slid down off the bed and propped myself up against the side of it, letting him sleep. The film traveled at a snail's pace, more drama than anything else, but I soon became engrossed in the story.

As the movie built to its climax, I kept moving closer and closer to the television, annoyed that he had known the ending but left me alone to experience it with no prior knowledge of the film. When it ended, with a real kick in the face, I started seething because he'd raved about it being such a good movie, but in the end it just left me feeling kinda empty.

Emptiness would be a luxury these days. Back then, we never worried then that anything we did might bring our deaths, or the death of the people we loved. Maybe that emptiness is what Jordan wanted.

When I snapped back to it, Brandon had finished smoking and everyone else had come outside.

"What's the plan then, Carson?" I asked.

He pointed to the main road. "We know that this road hits the highway, eventually. I say we follow it out until we hit the on ramp. When we get there, we'll stop and discuss the next steps."

"Affirmative," Brandon said.

"Got it," Alice said.

We climbed into our respective vehicles. Alice led the way in the jeep, Carson drove behind her in the pickup truck, and as per usual, Brandon and I brought up the rear.

I drove again, like always. The road leading to the

highway was oddly quiet, with little to no dead-nots staggering about. One or two runners chased after us, but we quickly lost them. Like anywhere else, bodies and abandoned vehicles lined the road.

It seemed strange to me. Maybe we'd moved too far away from civilization, or what remained of it. Maybe the dead-nots had finally started dying out. I didn't have a reasonable explanation for this. Only speculation.

Brandon and I passed most of the trip to the highway in silence. We looked for a white cars, anything resembling the one Jordan had taken off in. Vehicles, existing in various states of deterioration, dotted the roadside. Some had missing wheels, flat tires, or busted out windows. We didn't see another moving vehicle on the drive.

A little time passed before we reached the on ramp. Cars, abandoned after The Collapse, stood bumper to bumper at the entrance. When people had tried to get out of the city, I remember news reports discussing blockage on all major roadways and a ridiculous number of traffic accidents.

While most of the streets had vehicles off to the sides, the freeways and highways were a mess. One person or group of infected in the midst of those traffic jams bit people left and right, so we ended up with a fuck-ton of dead-nots that way.

Most of them had since wandered away from the road in search of fresh meat, but the vehicles remained packed like it was rush hour.

Some of us got out of the cars: Carson, Brandon,

Alice, Sarah, and me. We told each other the same story: no white vehicles, not even a hint of Jordan.

I shaded my eyes, looking out at the cars on the road. A light breeze blew through a maroon convertible with its top down. Hanging from the rearview mirror an air freshener, shaped like a red rose, twisted back and forth.

A revelation struck me then, and it surprised me that I hadn't thought of it before. "Carson, I think I know where Jordan went."

TWENTY

"WHAT? Why didn't you say something before?" Carson's voice rose with each word.

"I only just thought of it," I said, drawing circles in the ground with my boot.

"Well?" Carson's voice was tinged with impatience.

"The city rose garden. Franklin *loved* roses."

"Honestly Natalie, what makes you think that the rose garden won't be dead like everything else?" Alice asked.

"I don't know. It's just a hunch. To be honest, it's the best guess I got right now," I said.

"I suppose it's worth a shot," Sarah said.

"All right, Natalie," said Carson. "We'll give it a go. Keep this same formation on the drive to the rose garden."

So we piled back into the cars. Jordan's letter said he didn't want to be around anything that reminded him of Franklin, but it was all we had to go on. If we didn't find him there, I had no other ideas, so I kept telling myself that he had to be there. He *had* to.

I hadn't been on this side of town in a long time. Nestled in the heart of downtown amid tall buildings, sat the city rose garden, a well-loved place before The Collapse. Couples went on dates there, and people used it to escape, avoiding the rapid pace of the business district a couple of blocks away. They ate lunch in the picnic areas, sketched pictures of flowers, or chilled on one of the many benches scattered throughout the garden.

The garden spanned about five acres, at least. Anyone who lived here for some time knew it well with its some two hundred varieties of roses. Like other people, I'd been there many times before The Collapse. I remember the fragrance filling my nose every time I walked through it, the wave of pinks, reds, and yellows painting the grounds of the garden.

While I'd never been there with Brandon, I imagined that if we'd gone, it would have been with a picnic lunch and a book. We'd sit on a trademark checkered blanket, eat a whole spread of delicious foods. Cheese came to mind. I would lie in between his legs and read to him.

I'd gotten lost in my daydreams again, and the next thing I knew, Carson and Alice's vehicles had pulled into the entrance. From the large parking lot, I couldn't see much of the rose garden.

An air of calm permeated the area until I heard

Carson arguing with Chloe about staying in the pickup truck. She won the argument, of course. Pregnant or not, Chloe always did what she wanted. I admired her for that, wishing I had the courage to do whatever I wanted whenever I wanted.

Our steps rang out as we walked to the entrance of the garden. A wall the size of an average person surrounded it, and at its opening stood an even larger iron gate intricately interwoven with wrought iron roses. The gate, normally closed and locked, looked like it had been flung wide open.

We drew our edge weapons, on high alert. As we walked deeper into the garden, my mouth dropped open. It was in full bloom, every rosebush looking like it'd been maintained by a professional gardener. The garden teemed with red, pink, yellow, white, and orange roses.

"What the actual fuck?" I breathed.

"Oh my god, it's so beautiful!" Chloe said.

She stood in the middle of our group, almost as if we'd subconsciously formed a protective circle around her. A lone dead-not staggered toward us, and Carson jumped in front of it, shoving his blade up into its head via the neck.

With Carson on her heels, Chloe expressed a sudden need to pick a couple of roses in honor of Franklin, which I thought was not only pointless but also stupid.

Chloe ignored me when I mentioned this, and nicked herself while sawing at one of the stems with her knife, probably dull from use. A couple drops of blood shining crimson in the sunlight fell onto the roses, and after cussing and sticking her finger in her mouth, she finally gave up.

Deeper into the heart of the garden stood a white wooden gazebo with a brown roof and lattice work in between the columns. I remember it from my visits before The Collapse.

Inside the gazebo were benches, and around the outside, more rose bushes had been planted away from the path leading up to it. Anyone sitting in the gazebo could take in a three-hundred and sixty degree view of the garden, and it was always full of rose-lovers when there were still lots of people.

As we got closer to the gazebo, I saw a lone figure sitting there looking out at the garden. Jordan. I'd been right. I picked up my pace, reaching him before everyone else. He looked at me wide-eyed, as if I were a figment of his imagination.

Upon my approach, he released a heavy sigh. "Natalie?"

"I'm sorry, Jordan," I said.

"What are you doing here, Natalie? What are you all doing here?" He gestured to everyone now crowded behind me.

Never having been very good at confrontation, I released a sigh of relief when Carson spoke next. "You know we don't leave people behind, Jordan."

"Not even if they specifically requested to be left behind?" Jordan asked, voice terse.

He had a point there. Jordan *had* said that we shouldn't come after him. Yet, here we were, shoving our way into this introvert's space, trying to get him to come back with us.

I noticed he had a backpack. It lay open on the bench next to him, and books spilled out. Another book was flipped upside down near the pack. It definitely didn't look like fiction.

"What are you reading?" I asked, trying to change the subject.

With a blank stare, Jordan looked at the book and then back to me. "I doubt it would interest you. It's a book about the French Revolution."

Right on that account.

We sat still for a long time. I opened my mouth to say something but couldn't get any words out.

Jordan eventually broke the awkward silence. "It's quiet here, peaceful. Franklin truly loved this place. Besides our own backyard, this was his favorite place in the city. He brought me here on our first date sixteen years ago."

"I'm so sorry," I whispered.

"I thought about killing myself," Jordan's voice came out as a whisper, almost as if he didn't want to tell anyone this. "That thought plagued me so many times. Do you know what stopped me from doing it?"

"What?" I asked, picking at my nails.

"Franklin did. He would be so livid if we met in the afterlife because I had killed myself. I don't believe in God anymore. I stopped believing when I was a child. However, I truly believe that *something* happens to us when we die. I'm not sure exactly what that is, but I want to believe that we are perhaps reunited with our loved ones. I hope for that."

"I have no idea what happens either," I said. "But I think that's pretty beautiful."

I felt the need to hug him. I'd always been a hugger. When someone needed it, I wanted to wrap my arms around them. And maybe Jordan needed it at that moment.

Not leaving me much time to think about it, he reached over and hugged me. I responded by wrapping my arms around him. There was no sound for a while, but then his soft cry soon turned into muffled sobs.

When I pushed my hands into the back of his shirt in that embrace, I could feel that Jordan was covered in sweat. His shirt stuck to his back wherever I placed my hands. The morning chill was long gone.

It seemed strange to me that we'd worried so much about the weather getting colder. I guess that the recent heatwave plaguing the afternoon meant it was summer. I think things had just been nonstop for the longest time. No time to focus on the changing seasons.

Chloe dabbed her brow with the cutest purple handkerchief. As I looked at them, I noticed the rest of the group lingered in various states of discomfort. Beads of sweat dotted Carson's brow, which he wiped away with the back of his hand. Jordan's blue shirt had gone dark with large spots of perspiration.

Noises drew my attention away from my friends. I no longer saw the bright colors of the roses but the gray and blood-covered dead-nots that now surrounded the gazebo.

TWENTY-ONE

I SWALLOWED HARD, stretching my hand to tap Brandon or Carson or anyone but felt only dead air. Luckily, they'd already seen the dead-nots.

Carson tried to push Chloe behind him, but she shoved his arm away and drew her weapon. Seeing Chloe refuse to be treated like a helpless child when we all knew she could hold her own, especially with firearms and sharp objects, always made me happy.

When the dead-nots advanced on us, we drew our guns and started picking them off one by one. From the corner of my eye, I saw Chloe take out one after another. I hoped that made Carson feel dumb for treating her like a child earlier. Taking them out like this seemed to work well at first, and we paused for a moment to catch our breath and reload, all of us covered with sweat.

Looking over my shoulder, I saw that Jordan had backed up to the wall behind us because he was unarmed. Fuck. Why had he left without a weapon?

Foolish. I knew we had a couple of extra weapons in the cars, but I couldn't recall if anyone had any on them. Then I remembered that we'd brought fewer weapons than last time because we hadn't anticipated an attack of this magnitude.

Alice noticed Jordan didn't have a weapon and tossed him a camp knife. He caught it, a wave of relief spreading over his face.

But he didn't have time to use it. The wave of dead-nots, that had seemed to have come from nowhere, had suddenly ceased. Bodies of the dead-not-dead, now dead for real, dotted the area a short distance from the gazebo.

A light wind started up and stirred the overgrown grasses amid the bushes. The air was rich with the smell of perspiration and rose. The herbaceous smell of the grass, depressed beneath my feet, wafted into my nose too.

"We need to get out of here," Carson said.

"Good idea," said Brandon.

"Wait!" I said to Carson, and then turned to Jordan. "Jordan, come back with us."

"Natalie—"

But I cut him off. "Dude, I know you're hurting. I would be too. I can't say if I've ever loved anyone the way you loved Franklin, but if I lost the person I loved most in this world," I glanced over at Brandon, "it would legit kill me. But it can't hurt forever."

I didn't know for sure if Brandon was the love of my life, but I knew losing him would crush me. Brandon's eyes were hyper-focused on the surrounding area, so his didn't catch mine. He scanned from one end of the rose garden to the other, looking for any movement.

Jordan's brow furrowed. I hoped that meant he was contemplating my plea to come with us. I didn't think I could live with myself if I hadn't at least tried to get him to leave this place.

I reached out and gently wrapped my hand around his forearm, and then dragged my hand into his. I made my face soft, yet as imploring as possible.

"Please Jordan," I said again.

"Natalie," he said. "I am exhausted. I am so tired of everything. Of running from place to place, not putting roots down anywhere. I have grown weary of fighting dead-nots. But most of all, I no longer wish to live a life without Franklin."

"Jordan, we care about you. We're your friends," I said.

Jordan's eyes went wide. "Really Natalie? Tell me then, what do you know about me?"

I pushed out a breath. "I know you like tea and reading history books. I know your favorite novel is *Pride & Prejudice*. I know you prefer to be alone. Just because I don't know every detail about your life doesn't mean I don't care about you. We all care about you and want you to be, you know, not dead."

I placed my other hand on top of his, so that I was holding one of his hands with both of mine.

Jordan didn't have time to respond because gunshots broke the silence. Dead-nots had emerged again, this time in greater numbers. The sun beat down on us hard, reddening our already sweat-covered brows.

Our short reprieve over, we blew through one clip each, putting down the second round of dead-nots that had come for us. Grayed, decaying bodies littered the garden.

"Carson," Brandon said. "We need to move. Looks like they're gonna keep coming."

"Jordan," I said. "Please, no one wants to leave you here."

Finally, he gave me a single nod. I exhaled all the air I'd sucked into my lungs. It'd worked. He was going back with us.

We reloaded and started moving away from gazebo. Unfortunately, the ammo we had didn't match a mass of dead-nots this size. We'd only brought two clips each.

Eventually, we'd have to rely on our edge weapons to get us the fuck out of here. The dead-nots still advanced on us, now tumbling over the surrounding bodies stacked like sandbags. Some of the more frail ones had fallen while doing so and couldn't get back up, but those with any strength dragged themselves toward us.

Then came the runners, barreling our way, snarling like rabid dogs. There were so many now, so many. Even though we were still taking them down one by one, more continued moving toward us, some faster than others.

We looked around, unable to spot a place to break through them. I worried about ammunition, feeling pretty fucking hopeless right now. The circle around us grew with the regular slow-moving dead-nots, jumpers trying to bound over bodies, and runners trailing streams of bloody salvia as they careened toward us.

I was fucking scared. If anyone had asked me, I would've said, "I don't wanna die right now. No fucking way." I wanted to spend more time with these people, more time with Brandon.

Carson started shouting. He, Chloe, and Alice had carved a path for us to escape the gazebo area.

Blinded by the bright midday sunshine, we ran hard. As suspected, dead-nots followed us. They kept coming and coming. It seemed endless, but I couldn't let fear paralyze me. Not now. Not ever.

When we came upon the place where Chloe had tried to cut that rose earlier, we saw about six dead-nots there. One had fallen to its knees, gnawing on the ground.

Another dead-not had a crimson rose hanging from the side of its mouth like it had been chewing on it, the thorns slicing its lips and a stem poking out the side of its cheek. Its face was painted with jagged streaks of blood.

Carson ran up on the dead-not with the rose in its mouth, stabbing downward right into its skull. Then we each got in front of one of the others, making sure to brain stab 'em.

When we reached the gate, there must have been hundreds of them and who knows how many more behind the wall. They crawled and dove over one another, trying to get into the garden. Every once in a while, I saw the head of a jumper pop up like some freaky whack-a-mole.

Since we'd reloaded at the gazebo with the second of the two spare clips we each carried, I knew we were down to the last of our ammo. Switching to edge weapons would put us in close combat with hoards of dead-nots. I felt my stomach churn.

I wrestled with my stupid indecision once again. Should I continue to fire? Or should I start stabbing?

My eyes fell on each of my friends. Jordan gripped only an edge weapon and, by default, had been relegated to skull puncturing. Brandon preferred to use edge weapons in general, and I watched him kick and stab and kick and stab on a loop, never seeming to tire of killing dead-nots.

Chloe fired her gun while Carson switched between both his firearm and dagger. Alice and Sarah had a tag team method where one would minimize a threat from an oncoming dead-not, and the other would take it down for good.

I hesitated, my breathing unsteady. Why did everyone seem to have a handle on this situation except me?

All at once, the dead-nots, my friends, the roses, everything blurred together. I focused on the fence with its intricate, detailed iron roses, but I couldn't move, frozen in place. I remained unable to will my body to move in any direction.

"Natalie!" Carson yelled, breaking my zoning.

"Fuck." Releasing a breath, I drew my firearm and aimed.

It didn't matter how much we put them down, more kept coming, until we each had three or four dead-nots around us.

Moving toward the vehicles, Alice and Sarah put dead-nots down, maintaining their rhythm. I spotted Carson, Jordan, and Chloe a little farther away until Carson darted forward to take on five that were coming toward him, leaving Chloe and Jordan to work on their small batch alone. A ring of dead-nots encircled Brandon, and he went into berserker mode, summoning all his rage and channeling it into incredible strength.

After lunging at Jordan, a dead-not knocked him backward onto his ass. Chloe stood solo, alone to fight off three dead-nots. I'd cleaned my immediate area of threats. So I jumped over bodies, starting in her direction to help when I heard Brandon yelling. Not yelling for help. Brandon would never do that. It sounded more like the aggressive cry of one fighting off dead-nots that kept coming at him.

I stopped, unable to move in either direction. The moment was both infinite and instantaneous. My eyes drifted to Chloe. She'd taken out one of the three surrounding her in the time that passed. One of the other two, she kicked in the chest, and it went staggering backward like a drunk until it finally fell over. My eyes moved to Jordan, struggling with the one who had knocked him to the ground.

Meanwhile, dead-nots kept coming for Brandon,

like an endless wave. He kicked and stabbed, but it looked like their numbers had doubled. Chloe now turned around to assist the fallen Jordan.

The swell of dead-nots lessened. I looked at Brandon, stabbing skulls, and our eyes met. My head filled with pictures of us, memories, only the good ones. So I ran to him.

Together we decreased the number of dead-nots moving toward us.

A brief moment of relief washed over me, and I wanted to jump into his arms, wrap my legs around his waist, and kiss him harder than I'd ever kissed anyone.

But a scream from Chloe ripped through the air, and my heart dropped into my gut. I couldn't seem to turn any faster than in slow motion. A chill spread through the air, and I shivered as I focused on the situation.

Chloe kicked a dead-not who'd sunken its teeth into her beautiful calf. It rolled over. With her good leg, she stomped on its head. She gave a satisfied half-smile at the snap and the crunch. Then, looking woozy, she fell. Jordan moved to catch her, and tears spilled from her eyes.

Chloe's scream had jarred Carson. He shoved a dead-not backward into a couple of others, knocking them down like dominoes. He leapt over bodies as his eyes met mine, and I'd never seen more blame on someone's face in my entire life. Tears rolled down my cheeks in steady streams.

Carson cut a path with his remaining bullets until

he reached Chloe, shouting her name until his voice went hoarse. He scrambled over the last few bodies, and when he reached her, knelt down on the side opposite Jordan. Carson pulled Chloe's body into his.

Alice yelling "Fire in the hole!" shattered any moment we had to process what had just happened.

Carson picked Chloe up like she was made of glass and jogged away from the gate. Jordan, Brandon, and I booked it hard. As soon as we'd cleared the area, I heard the clink of a grenade as it bounced right into the open gate. And then it blew.

The impact threw dead-not bodies in every direction, clearing a path for us back to the vehicles. While it hadn't killed every single one in our way, it had stunned those remaining. They staggered around for a short time as if trying to reorient themselves before they started moving our way again.

But we'd made it to the vehicles. I climbed into the sports car, feeling sick.

Even though I didn't wanna face what came next, I'd never been happier to leave a rose garden in my entire life.

TWENTY-TWO

WHEN WE GOT BACK to the warehouse store, it was eerily silent. Upon exiting the pickup truck, Carson slammed the driver's side door. His footfalls were heavy as he walked to the passenger's side to help Chloe. When he opened her door, she pitched forward into his arms.

He didn't close the truck door, so Alice jogged over and shut it. She wrapped her arm around Sarah as they walked inside. Jordan followed until Brandon and I stood alone in the parking lot. The sun edged toward the horizon.

We grabbed our stuff and walked back inside the building. Inside, Carson had laid Chloe on a large bed. He left her a moment before returning to her side with a bottle of clear alcohol, a towel, and a bandage. When the alcohol hit her skin, she let out a sharp bird-like cry.

When he'd finished cleaning and bandaging her, he wound his arms around her. His embrace looked like someone holding a fragile thing. They stayed together, locked in this embrace.

The horrible truth stirred in my stomach like bile. Chloe didn't have much time left before she turned. But no one would dare confront Carson with a fact he already knew. We left them to have their remaining time together.

Brandon laid hands on my shoulders and guided me toward our blanket fort.

My stomach lurched. I was responsible for this. The choice I'd made to leave her and help Brandon caused her death. I tore myself away from him and ran through the back door, where I threw up in one of the overgrown bushes surrounding the back lot.

I wiped my face. I hated vomiting in general, but the sour tang that lingered on my tongue sucked most of all. But not as much as it'd suck to live with what I'd done.

When I turned around, Jordan stood behind me. "It was not your fault, Natalie."

"What?" I said, trying to ignore the elephant in the warehouse store.

"What happened to Chloe, it was not your fault," he said.

Clutching my stomach, I walked over to the side of the building and slid down it into a sitting position. Jordan joined me.

"I fucked up, Jordan, big time."

"There was no conceivable way you could have predicted what would happen. Brandon was surrounded. You thought you were doing the right thing. Life is full of choices. We make the choice we deem the best in the moment. Sometimes, the consequences are good. Sometimes, they are bad. More often than not, we will not know the consequences of our actions until much later. You did something that you thought was the right thing. If it were me, I would have chosen to assist Franklin over any of you." His eyes sparkled with tears.

"I don't think I can ever forgive myself. I killed her, Jordan. She's dead because of me." I rolled my tongue around, trying to get the taste of vomit out of my mouth. "And her baby—"

"You, *you* didn't kill anyone," he said. "A dead-not did."

I put one hand to my head, followed by the other, and dragged them through my hair. I didn't know how to fix this in my head, unable to stop blaming myself for what had happened to Chloe. If I thought too hard about it, I probably never could.

"I'll never forgive myself," I whispered.

"I think you should speak to her," Jordan said.

I looked at him wide-eyed. He tapped my shoulder and nodded his head to the door as if to say that I should walk my ass back into this warehouse store and make my peace with what happened to Chloe before she died. The only way to do that was to talk to her.

I didn't answer him. Instead, I got up and walked back inside, the very act taking more courage than I've ever had to summon before.

The quiet of the interior overwhelmed me at once.

Absent were the familiar sounds of the children play-ing. I couldn't see anyone, and it seemed like the only thing in the entire warehouse store was Chloe on the bed and Carson sitting next to her. Emptiness had seeped into every corner.

I walked toward her, feeling like I'd rather sink to the bottom of the ocean. But it felt like I was sinking now, as pressure assaulted my ears the way the depth of the water made it impossible for any sounds to penetrate it.

Sweat covered Chloe's face, and her beautiful terra-cotta skin had lost its color. She still looked beautiful though. No matter what Chloe looked like, she would always be gorgeous to me.

Before I could open my mouth, Carson got so close to my face, his hot breath stung my skin. "God-dammit, Natalie, you better back up."

"Carson." Chloe coughed his name out. "Leave her alone . . . please."

Carson looked at me like he wished I would shrivel up and die right in front of him. My breathing grew rough, but I stood my ground until he finally moved around me. He would never ignore Chloe's wishes, especially not as she lay dying.

The walk to the bed seemed endless. As I got closer, I could see tiny gray patches which had formed in small circles on her face, like dead-not pimples. Her veins were more pronounced. She was turning quicker than I thought. A couple of hours or an eternity had passed. I couldn't be sure.

I sat on the bed next to her, the spot still warm

from where Carson had been moments ago. She reached out her cold and clammy hand, and I placed mine inside it.

"I'm so sorry, Chloe," I murmured.

"Natalie, you dummy, I don't blame you," she said. "I love you."

"I love you too, Chloe. You always helped me try to see this world as not such a bad place."

"But so stubborn, you still wanted to see it as bad," she said.

I tried to laugh, but a squeak came out amid the tears now pouring from my eyes. She inhaled a ragged breath and coughed a little. Carson, standing nearby, eyed us. She held up her hand in his direction as if indicating that she was fine . . . for now.

"I'm so sorry. I am so sorry." I emphasized each word, unable to stop apologizing. "Your baby—"

"Natalie." She blew out a heavy breath. "It wasn't your fault. You didn't bite me."

This time, I did snort out a tiny laugh before wrapping my arms around her. "I'll never forget you."

"You better not or I'll haunt you," she said. "Now go tell my angry boyfriend to get back over here."

I kissed her forehead and got up, dragging my hand from hers until only our fingers touched, and then I let go. I nodded to Carson. I silently passed him because I was pretty sure that he didn't wanna talk to me at all. He walked back to the bed and sat next to Chloe.

I watched them for a long time. I'd never seen Carson cry, but now tears spilled from his eyes and streaked down his hard cheekbones as they talked in whispers. After what felt like an eternity, he lifted his blade, moving it close to Chloe's head, but his hand didn't stop shaking. Chloe put one weak hand over his, as if trying to steady him.

But he fumbled and dropped the blade. He bent over her body, and choked sobs came from his muffled mouth. They grew louder, loud enough to rouse the dead-not-dead. But I doubt he cared. I wouldn't have cared if that were me bent over Brandon. After several more failed attempts, it became clear that Carson couldn't do it.

I looked at Brandon, a silent plea forming behind my eyes. I couldn't do it either. Tears dropped to my shirt, and I swear between Carson and me, we could've filled oceans. Brandon didn't need an explanation. His hands went around his camp knife, and the sound of him unsheathing it was almost as loud as metal going through bone.

Without a word to me or anyone, Brandon moved to the bed. He hovered near it for a long time before determination seemed to grab hold of him, and he clapped his hand on Carson's shoulder. Still bent over Chloe sobbing, Carson stiffened, but when she stroked his hair, his body relaxed.

I moved closer to Brandon, not close enough to touch him. The thought of watching him kill Chloe caused acid to rise up my throat. I argued with myself, losing to the voice that said watching Chloe die would be my punishment for fucking everything up.

Brandon tightened his grip on Carson's shoulder, moving him toward Chloe's hip rather than her stomach and chest. Carson looked like he tried to get ahold of himself, wiping his face and nose. He sat up and gripped Chloe's hand.

Dropping to his knees, Brandon wove his hand under Chloe's head. For a long time, he couldn't move his other hand. But it eventually happened by degrees. At his side. On the bed. Next to Chloe's shoulder. I couldn't breathe. His hand remained steady as he raised the knife up and then brought it down next to her head. He couldn't do it either. I didn't expect this. He and Chloe were never close.

I swallowed several times, worrying I might have to do it. I couldn't. I couldn't. I just couldn't do it. Chloe touched Brandon's knife hand softly, and her eyes bore into his. She whispered something and then nodded at him. Finally, she jutted her chin out before closing her eyes.

The whole warehouse store seemed to go dark. Brandon finally brought the knife down into Chloe's forehead. A low gurgle bubbled from her throat. Her body shook and then went still.

The sound of Carson's sobs as he collapsed onto her filled the entire place. I squeezed my eyes shut as the tears fell, unable to look at the sadness all over the faces of my friends.

TWENTY-THREE

AFTER CHLOE'S DEATH, I couldn't be sure if one hour or several hours had passed.

Carson started throwing over random pieces of furniture and smashing glassware. He'd always been level-headed, the one telling us to be quiet, but now he didn't care at all.

And me? Well, I hadn't thrown anything. But I cared about Chloe, my friend and former lover. She didn't deserve such a horrific fate. Neither had Franklin, or Omar and Kelsey, but the ghosts of our group would haunt me forever. None of us deserved this shithole world we'd been forced to call home.

Carson held a bottle of clear liquor in one hand and knocked some boxes off a nearby shelf, kicking them when they tumbled in front of him. He dragged himself to the back door, pushing it open with more force than necessary. Jordan jogged after him. I couldn't hear what he said to Carson, but soon both of them disappeared out of sight.

When Carson returned, Jordan followed at his heels. The rest of us had gathered around the big table in the middle of the store, stewing in uncomfortable silence.

As they walked toward us, Jordan pleaded with Carson. "Please Carson, this will solve nothing."

Brandon got to his feet in front of Carson. "Can I help you?"

"Get out of my goddamn way," Carson said. "Or I will make you."

Carson shoved all his weight into Brandon. Brandon stumbled backward and fell. He immediately jumped back to his feet but not before Carson ripped me out of my chair, bringing me to face him.

Everyone else got up and huddled around Carson. I let out a yelp as Carson twisted his hand around my shirt, choking me with my own clothes.

"Carson, what the fuck?" I forced out the words.

Alcohol wafted from his breath, sour on my face. Jordan grabbed a hold of Carson's forearm, trying to pry me out of his hands. Carson didn't budge, and now the crescendo of voices rose through the store. From the corner of my eye, I spotted Brandon walking over to our blanket fort.

"Carson, let her go! Please! It wasn't her fault," Jordan said.

"Why are you doing this, Carson?" Alice shouted.

Carson didn't respond to either of them, and a fire burned behind his eyes, looking like they were about to spill flames right onto me. Words couldn't touch him. Reason couldn't touch him.

My eyes watered, my words strained as I clawed at Carson's hand. "Carson . . . Brandon . . . "

Carson tightened his fist, and with his other hand, he unholstered his gun. He lifted it to my temple.

Alice and Sarah, still shouting, kept their distance, and I heard them tell Steve and Naomi to "keep the children away from here." Brandon returned, and when he approached Carson, Carson turned his weapon on Brandon. I hoped to pass out, so I wouldn't have to see whatever loomed on the horizon.

"I will fucking end you," Brandon said, pointing his gun at Carson.

"You going to shoot me first or am I going to shoot you first?" Carson asked, his voice gritty and low.

"That depends on whether or not you let her go," Brandon said.

"This is preposterous!" Jordan said. "Stop this! We are friends. She is your friend."

"I should kill you," Carson said to Brandon. "Her obsession with you caused her to leave Chloe alone. She's dead because of you two."

My body teetered on numbness.

Rude, I thought. Not obsessed with Brandon.

Things went fuzzy.

"Carson, please," Jordan said. "No one is at fault for Chloe's death. If anything, it is this world. This world is killing us. We cannot continue fighting like this, or we will never survive."

I started to lose consciousness until the sound of

Akira gurgling shook Carson. He let me go, and my head hit the ground hard. And everything went black.

TWENTY-FOUR

THE NIGHT AIR nipped at my cheeks, and I pulled my coat tighter around my chest. It'd been days, or maybe weeks even since I'd told Brandon that Carson could go fuck himself.

That night after Carson choked me, I decided I had no desire to hang around anyone who wanted me dead, and as soon as I came to, Brandon found me in our blanket fort packing a bag.

"Fuck that fucking asshole," I said.

I'd shoved my combat gear and clothes ripped from the shelves of the warehouse store into a backpack. I tore through paper boxes of granola bars, dumping them in there too.

"You gonna bounce?" Brandon asked.

"You better fucking believe it." I huffed, rubbing my hand across my neck; no one would ever put their hands on me like that again.

"I wanna be somewhere quiet. I daydream about a

home far away from stupid dead-nots and bitches yelling," Brandon said.

I stopped packing and looked at him. "Does that mean—"

"Let's go." He cut me off before I could finish.

"You mean I don't have to drag you with me like last time?"

"Negative. If I stay here, I'll prolly murder Carson. I always feel like murder these days," Brandon murmured.

I put my arms around him, and he moved my body close to his. "I talked to Alice, privately. She said I could take the weapons I had on me, and some ammo and that she wouldn't mind parting with the sports car."

"Dope." He pressed his face into my hair, followed by a quick kiss. "No way I'd leave without my blades. Holding that wakizashi still makes me get tight in the pants."

"Good, then pack a bag, and let's get the fuck out of here."

It didn't take us long to get sorted, and I took the books and twinkle lights for nostalgia's sake. The memories of being in this blanket fort reading with Brandon were the best ones I'd had to date. Ever since we went on the run, things had gotten worse. I, too, wanted to be somewhere quiet.

Emerging from our makeshift home, I saw the shadow of darkness had settled onto the warehouse store. Carson lay sprawled on the bed, passed out. Alice and Sarah sat at the table, cooking something rich-smelling over the propane stove. I could see no one else.

As I got close, a hint of something sweet filled my nostrils. It looked like baked beans.

"Hey Natalie, Brandon." Alice looked at us, loaded up with stuffed backpacks. "Take care of yourselves, all right?"

I pressed my palm into Alice's warmly. "Thank you, Alice, for everything."

Brandon nodded a silent thanks, and we turned to leave.

"Before you go," Sarah said.

We stopped and spun around to face her, and she handed Brandon a bottle of triple blend aged Irish whiskey.

A big, goofy smile spread across Brandon's face. "Thanks lady."

"Never know when that might come in handy, and it's the best we got here. Be safe," Sarah said.

I smiled and gave half a wave, a bit sad to say goodbye to two of the coolest chicks I'd ever met.

The air outside blew into our faces when we opened the door, cooler than I'd thought it'd be. I guess the oppressive heat wave we'd been slammed with at the rose garden had blown out of here.

Brandon had already gotten it to the car, when I spotted Jordan in the doorway of the warehouse store. He called me back. In my hurry to leave, I'd forgotten that he deserved a goodbye too.

"Natalie," Jordan said.

"Jordan," I said, trying to match his seriousness.

"Your decision to leave astounds no one, but I wanted to say farewell unless we never meet again. If I may leave you with some parting words?"

I nodded.

"My favorite thing about love is that is wears many faces. It is a magnificent and powerful thing. Everyone deserves a love like Franklin and I had, but no one deserves to be taken advantage of because of their love."

This time I hugged him. "Take care of yourself, Jordan."

"You as well," he said.

Inside the sports car, I removed the Bowie knife from my belt, as I'd always done every time I got into a car, wedging it between the seat and the center console.

I clicked the buckle of the seatbelt. "Where to?"

With a crinkling sound Brandon removed something from his back pocket. He passed the paper to me, a map. Steve's map, to be more specific.

"Where did you get this?" I whispered.

"Took it from the guy I gut-stabbed at the hospital. He must've got it from Carson."

The map looked like it had been torn from an atlas or something and detailed the woods surrounding the city, the words "Summer Camp" scrawled above them.

Summer Camp claimed to be a walled fortress, a literal summer camp that survivors had built a high fence around, high enough to protect its inhabitants from dead-nots. Provided they were free of bites, anyone with a map to Summer Camp would be welcomed in and offered lodging in return for helping the community. It was Steve and everyone else's fabled mecca.

"Summer Camp," I mused, starting the car. "I never thought this was real. I thought we'd been everywhere in the city, but I guess we never ventured out this far."

"Guess not," Brandon said with a shrug.

"Okay, let's do it."

On the road, we passed an uncountable number of abandoned vehicles. The path to Summer Camp was rumored to be unpaved, and we'd need an SUV to better get us deep into the forest.

Brandon and I decided to drive the sports car until it ran out of gas or we came across a car dealership, whichever came first.

Now, the night air nipped at my cheeks, and I pulled my coat tighter around my chest. Brandon had his arm wrapped around my shoulder, and we leaned against the car looking at the stars. White wisps of smoke curled into the air, and at every inhale the ember at the end of his cigarette glowed bright orange against the black sky.

The sounds of rustling leaves filled the air, and when they stilled, I could hear frogs singing or crickets chirping. Fucking peaceful.

This might've been what Brandon had wished for. I'd never considered myself much of a nature girl, but I could get used to this kind of quiet.

TWENTY-FIVE

UNABLE TO BREATHE, I couldn't stop running. I tried to keep close to Brandon. Since he had a lead on me, every so often he'd stop and fire over my head.

The used car lot we'd found had been crawling with dead-nots, but we had no choice. The fuel gauge pushed on empty, and I'd been watching it drop like a countdown clock for a while.

While still in the car, I distracted a group of them by honking the horn, and Brandon popped out the window and picked some off. Alice had been more than generous, letting him take the assault rifle.

When we finally ran out of gas, I let the car roll to a stop, and then we jumped out and took off running. Never being much of a runner, I thought I couldn't keep it up much longer. I envied Brandon's long legs, and it surprised me that someone who smoked so much could run like he did.

We'd lured the remaining dead-nots away from the used car lot, the runners gaining on us faster than the stragglers, so we shot at them first. We hadn't seen any jumpers this time, so we lucked out when none of them sprung on us.

Now Brandon pointed toward a thicket of trees, and I ran into them while he kept to the main road. Three dead-nots went after him and four with me. Great.

I stopped running to catch my breath, and when a runner came at me faster than the others, I kicked it over. It fell back, its body twisting in some exposed roots. The thing spat blood and snarled, and I moved to it, put my boot on its chest, and buried my Bowie knife into its skull.

I stood panting for a moment. And then, after sucking in a deep breath, I took off again, using the trees as obstacles. Since I'd put down the runner, I'd lucked out with the other three that were slower dead-nots. Grateful for that, for not needing to sprint, I slowed down to a jog.

Brandon better hurry his ass up getting his dead-nots good and dead, I thought.

My break over, they'd gained on me again, and I used a low branch to closeline one of them. Looking like it walked on a treadmill, it reached over the branch, trying to grab me but unable to move forward.

The other two split left, following me through another obstacle course of trees. I spun around and fired toward one's head, but as it turned to snarl at me, it dodged the bullet, which hit its taller companion in the shoulder. Fresh, thick, almost black blood spilled from the wound.

"Fuck," I muttered.

Since I'd emptied the magazine, I didn't have time to reload. I wanted to shout out to Brandon for help, but I didn't wanna rouse anymore dead-nots. It looked like some good old-fashioned hand-to-hand combat.

I let them come for me, super thankful for my thick clothing. When the closer one reached out toward me, I dropped to the ground, grabbed its leg, and sliced its Achilles tendon. It crumpled at once. I left it to squirm around on the forest floor while I took care of the other.

The other dead-not lunged at me, probably pissed because I'd shot it in the shoulder. I finally looked at the thing. It must have stood well over six-feet tall, built like a brick house. How the actual fuck would I put down this beast? Also, why was this literal body-builder hanging out in a middle-of-nowhere car dealership?

I spotted his name tag, hanging askew on his too-tight polo shirt. "Ted" and above that "1000 Smiles Automobile." Too bad Ted had no more smiles for any of us. The behemoth lurched at me, causing me to stumble. If I fell and this monster fell on me, I'd prob-ably be as good as dead.

Wait, I had an idea. A risky idea, but an idea nonetheless. What if I fell? What if I fell on purpose, my Bowie knife standing straight up? And what if Ted fell onto my knife?

I'd have to line up everything perfectly. Ted would have to fall with his chompers heading straight for my head or neck.

The forest opened up into a small clearing. Nice. Even ground would be better for my theatrical fall.

Ted came crashing through the opening in a spray of leaves. He growled like a mother bear warning people away from her cubs. Drool mixed with blood trailed down his chin in streams.

His polo shirt looked like it could have been white at one time. Now it was motley, with yellow, brown, green, black, and blood-red stains.

I sprinted into the clearing. "Come on, fucker."

Biting down hard, I unsheathed my Bowie knife and fell backward, arms splayed like I was Jesus on the cross. After that bit of flair, I put my fists together, cupping one over the other that held tight to the upward-pointing Bowie knife.

My knuckles went white as Ted ambled closer to me. Before I knew it, he towered over me, his giant form blocking out the sun. He spit white foam and blood bubbly with saliva before roaring. I blinked rapidly a couple of times and the next thing I knew, he'd dropped to his knees on the side of me. He hadn't collapsed on top of me like I'd hoped. Trust good ol' Natalie to fuck this one up, too. I rolled away the moment Ted reached for me.

I scrambled up and leapt onto Ted's back. He tried

to buck me off like a wild horse, but I gripped hard as he whipped his body from side-to-side. I used the brief moment he stopped his erratic movements to drive my Bowie knife into his skull. Ted crumbled to the ground, and I swear, had anyone been standing there, they would have shaken from the tremor of his fall.

Panting, I squeezed my eyes shut, and climbed off the downed beast. Falling to my knees and then rolling onto my back, I laid there for what felt like an eternity, trying to regulate my breathing.

When I could finally get back on my feet, my whole body ached. I walked back to the road, every step taking way too much effort.

Reaching the road, I didn't see Brandon anywhere. "Where the fuck you at?"

I'd run a little far away from the car lot, and I could see the sports car in the distance. Walking into the middle of the road, I tried to see another person, and saw no one, dead-not-dead or alive.

The screech of tires rang through the air, and I snapped my head around to see an SUV slam into some dead-nots in the used car lot and barrel down the road toward me. I jumped to the side of the road.

Window rolled down, the SUV came to a stop and Brandon stuck his head out. "Going my way, sweets?"

"Are you fucking serious right now? Where were you the whole time?" I narrowed my eyes at him.

"Getting this." He tapped his hand on the side of the vehicle.

After climbing in the passenger seat, I slapped his arm. "Thanks for your help"

"I figured you had it under control."

"Let's go, asshole." My breathing finally normalized, but my heart gave a little flutter as he wrapped his hand around mine.

TWENTY-SIX

THE DIRT ROAD SEEMED ENDLESS. I hoped this was the right one. It was where the map and a marker on the side of the road had led us. This *had* to be it.

During the drive, Brandon talked a bit about wobbly black holes. A couple times he tried to get handsy, but instead of pulling the car over to the side of the road to have a quickie, I moved his hand into mine or just off of me completely.

To be honest, I hadn't felt very amorous since Chloe had died and Carson had choked the shit outta me while saying I was obsessed with Brandon.

I was *not* obsessed with Brandon. Brandon was like a light fixture. In that, most people ignored it until it blew, right? He was always there, hovering in the periphery of my life.

Okay, fine, I went looking for him when The Collapse first happened, but that wasn't the same as obsessed. It wasn't like I was drawing his name surrounded by hearts in my kitten notebook. Shit. I'd have to check the kitten notebook.

Jordan's words also stung. Was he trying to say that I kept giving Brandon everything while he gave me nothing? That wasn't true. Brandon gave me warm fuzzy feelings.

After what seemed like a million years of driving, we came to a high fence. It looked solid, but made up of a patchwork of various pieces of metal and wood.

Bullseye. No summer camp I knew had a prison fence around it.

Hanging sideways, as if it had fallen and been rehung one too many times, a sign read Camp Dewsmile. What a weird name. It looked like something from the 1970s with its sun washed coloring and archaic bubble letters carved into a plank of wood. A faded pink smiley face stared at us from the inside the D.

Brandon stopped the SUV a short distance away from it. Nothing happened. The gate didn't move.

"What do we do?" I asked, looking at Brandon.

He shrugged. "Go say hello?"

He moved to get out of the vehicle, but I grabbed his arm. "Are you sure?"

Brandon looked at me like I'd just pissed on his shoe. "Why not?"

Shaking himself free of me, he opened the door, the automatic rifle slung over his shoulder.

"Hello . . . " Brandon's "oh" sounded more like "ew."

I lingered in the car a moment before getting out. "Is there a secret code word or something?"

A head popped up from the fence, aiming a weapon at us. "Identify yourselves!"

Brandon and I threw our hands up, but I spoke first, afraid his tendency to be abrasive might cause us to get shot. "Hey, yo, hi. I'm Natalie, and this is Brandon."

Brandon didn't bother to wave.

The fence man had an unnecessarily loud and aggressive voice. "What are you doing here?"

"So we have this map." I gestured to my back pocket. "Is it okay if I — "

"Turn around and grab it!"

Calm down, sir. Whatever. I did as he asked and spun with my hands raised before I put my hand in my back pocket, extracting the map. I unfolded it and turned back around, holding it high above my head.

The man looked at it through a scope on his rifle.

"All right! It looks like a legitimate map!"

I dropped my shoulders in relief. *Good. Let's get through this fucking gate.*

Brandon and I moved back to the SUV.

"Hold it!" The man guarding the wall went back to shouting, or maybe he never stopped shouting. "Before we let you in, we need you to strip!"

My whole body bristled. "Excuse me?"

I looked wide-eyed at Brandon, who'd already dropped his pants.

"What?" He now pulled his shirt over his head.

I glared up at the man. "Why do you want us naked, you perv?"

"We're not pervs! People hide bites all the time! We just want to see that you've not been bitten!"

How humiliating. Well, what better way to meet our new neighbors, I thought as I removed my clothing.

When we got the all-clear from the fence man, the gate opened toward us, two people pushing it forward. They closed it as soon as we got the SUV in. Another person appeared and directed us to park the SUV near some other vehicles by the gate.

A woman, who reminded me a lot of Alice, jogged over to us after we'd climbed out of the SUV. She had dark hair, cut short, spiking in every direction. She wiped her hands on her dark blue jeans and stuck one out for a shake.

"Hey there," she said, her East Coast accent coloring her words. "Sorry about all the fuss out there. We gotta make sure there ain't nobody bringin' zombies in here. I'm Queenie."

"Natalie." I pointed to myself and then gestured at Brandon. "Brandon."

"You hungry?" Queenie asked.

"I could eat," I said.

"Yup," Brandon said.

The camp was bigger inside than it looked from the outside. A bunch of raised cabins lined the inside of the fence, and tons of people mulled about. Queenie led us to a building much larger than the cabins with a sign out front, carved like the one hanging outside the camp, that said "Smile Dining."

"They're big on smiles here," I whispered to Brandon.

"I got smiles for you." Brandon gave me a big dopey grin then, and I almost forgot I hadn't wanted him to touch me.

Inside Smile Dining were several long tables standing end to end, some empty while others had people sitting eating bowls of food or playing cards. A few people fell to hushed whispers when we walked by, but most ignored us.

Queenie guided us to an empty table where other people brought us piping hot bowls of food, piled high. I dug my nose into the smells wafting from the dishes. PB&Js be damned! Real fucking food.

"Dewsmile was a real lucky find. The kitchen was fully stocked like they was preparin' for camp when everythin' went to hell," Queenie said "Don't know if they was ever campers in here or not, but it was empty when we found it. We built this fence around the perimeter after we'd cleared the camp of some crawlies who must've wandered in here. Been here ever since. We go out once in a while to search for food or weapons. But mostly we stay here.

"Eat up, and then we'll take you over to Sunshine, where you can get some rest. You look exhausted. In the mornin', we'll give you the lay of the land. We run Dewsmile like a community, meanin' everyone pulls their weight around here. We'll give you more details and see what you can do after you've had some sleep."

Brandon and I ate some stew or something, and

then Queenie escorted us to the cabins. Ours was called Sunshine Smile and had a worn carving of a grinning sun. Queenie passed me a gas lantern, and said goodnight.

Inside were four bunk beds. It felt like we were actually going to camp. Each bed had a plastic mattress and a blanket with no pillows or sheets. Though compared to how we'd slept in the past—on the floor of a jail cell, on the floor of a warehouse store —this seemed like luxury.

"Sweet," I said. "Bunk beds. Top or bottom?"

"Seeing that heat rises, the gentlemen thing to do is take the top and later drop."

I guess he anticipated spending plenty of hot summer days in here.

"Into my bunk?" I could feel the heat creeping up my neck into my ears.

"Of course," he said.

It looked like no one else occupied this cabin, which meant I was doomed to succumb to Brandon's charms. When he dropped into my bunk, he'd have me naked before too long. While I totally wanted that, I also didn't want it at the same time.

Dammit Jordan. And stupid fucking Carson. Fuck that guy. Why did I care about what some guy, who'd choked the shit out of me, had to say? Sure he'd known me for a while, but he didn't know me like Brandon did, and if I'd asked Brandon, I doubt he'd say I was obsessed with him. But I probably shouldn't have been asking anyone but myself if it was true.

TWENTY-SEVEN

IN THE MORNING, Queenie continued the tour, and we got a proper look at the camp for the first time. It was far bigger than the brief glimpse we'd gotten last night. Besides the cafeteria, there was a huge firepit dead center of the camp.

Near the front gate, the place with the most sunshine, a vegetable garden burst with budding plants. Not too far from that was a chicken coop, and they had a couple of cows and pigs. I even spotted a rooster hopping around. I had a feeling we'd be eating eggs for breakfast, and I looked forward to that again.

The fence met the edge of a lake that stretched farther than I could see. It had a small wooden dock with a rowboat tied there. This place really was a legit summer camp and reminded me of the joy I had during the years I was a Girl Scout. I went to camp every year and had a blast. My moment of nostalgia got slapped away by the fact that dead-nots weren't trying to devour my flesh back then, but they defi-nitely were now.

The tour stopped back at the cafeteria, and Queenie said we should help ourselves to breakfast. I don't think I could possibly describe the spread. Fresh vegetables and fruit, scrambled eggs, milk and cereal. Cereal!

I didn't wanna be too greedy, but I also wanted to load my plate with everything in front of me. In the end, I settled on an apple, cereal, and scrambled eggs with onions and peppers.

Brandon and I sat at one of the empty community tables, and Queenie sat across from us without a plate of food. She wiped a red apple on her shirt, and the crunch from her first bite echoed throughout the cafe-teria. She chewed almost methodically without taking her eyes off of us and didn't speak until she swallowed.

"So kids, what can you do?"

Eyebrow raised, I looked at her before remem-bering she was referring to the community program they had going on here.

"I'm not too bad at cooking," I said.

Sighing heavily after that, I thought about my unicorn notebook, lost forever. I'd tried to recreate the cooking tips Franklin had given me, but in the end, I couldn't recall even half of the things I'd written in it. The kitten notebook was a mere shell of the unicorn one.

Queenie swallowed another bite of apple. "That's perfect. Mariana and Hector could use some help in the kitchen. How 'bout you?"

"I guess I gotta be on defense, weapons and shit," Brandon said, dumping hot sauce onto his eggs.

"You think you'd benefit us most there?" Queenie asked.

"Long as no one talks to me," Brandon said.

I snickered, guessing Brandon didn't plan to make any new friends.

"That's fair," Queenie said. "Natalie, I'll introduce you to Mariana and Hector. Brandon, you can report to Jae at the gate. I'll be back to fetch you after breakfast. Enjoy."

Queenie got up from the table, leaving Brandon and I to eat in peace. I hadn't slept well last night. As he'd said, Brandon had evacuated his bunk and snuggled up next to me in mine last night. Not too long after he'd pressed his body into mine, I'd felt him somewhere else pressed hard into me, too.

So many conflicting feelings bubbled inside me about having sex with him. I wanted to, but I also didn't want to, fearing it'd shatter the comfortable pattern we'd settled into. More than that, I feared he'd run away, leaving me heartbroken again.

In the end, we fucked. After a lot of kissing and teasing, it just seemed like the natural progression of things. Plus, we were finally alone for once. What else could I do? I never could say no to Brandon, no matter how many conflicting feelings I had. But not like I wanted to anyway.

Though it felt amazing, emotionally it didn't have the intended effect, leaving me with more questions than answers. When he fell asleep shortly after, the only thing I could do was stare at the top bunk, trying to count the lines in the wood.

I'd thought about having Brandon that way again for so long. Why did I suddenly feel like I'd made the whole wrong choice? It should've been a victory. I'd won. Natalie got Brandon. Finally. Instead of being dopey happy, I felt like I'd made a huge mistake.

What if Carson had been right? What if Chloe's death *had* been my fault? Blinders. I always had blinders on when it came to Brandon. He was all I could ever see.

And what if Jordan was right too? Had I really loved Brandon no matter what? And was that the best thing?

At that moment, I really hated myself, but I couldn't even squeeze out one tear. I felt numb.

The next morning, I poked at my eggs, disappointed in myself for the sudden loss of appetite. I looked at Brandon, sitting next to me his greasy hair tucked under a baseball cap, t-shirt hugging his wiry frame.

Fuck, he was hot. Get your shit together, Natalie.

He bumped my shoulder playfully, and it broke me out of my wallowing trance.

"You done?" I looked at his empty plate.

"Yup, may go back for seconds. May get to fucking up some dead-nots."

"Whatever makes you happy."

"You make me happy," he said, nudging me again.

Warmth spread through my face, and I smiled like

a big dumb animal. Yes Brandon, take me. Take my body and soul. Whatever you need, it's yours.

"I adore you like crazy." I pushed in closer to him, unable to resist the gravitational pull.

"Don't start. Got work to do. Community and all," he said.

"Right, get to work then."

"And you can imagine me poking you sensitively in your squishy bits."

"I think the memory is still fresh enough." I couldn't help but smile at him.

Brandon pressed his lips to the top of my head and walked toward the cafeteria door before I could even say goodbye. As I watched him go, I felt an ache.

Brandon festered like a disease, consuming my body, taking over, and putting all of himself into me. For this parasite, I was only a host, a shell, and I swore I could physically feel how he'd attached himself to me. And then in his absence, I felt empty. A longing to run after him swirled around in my gut.

I looked down at my barely eaten breakfast. It had always been my favorite meal of the day before all this shit. I hunched over, angry at myself for slugging through life as a sack of conflicting emotions.

The eggs in my mouth now tasted like mush, unlike when I'd taken my first bite. What was wrong with me?

Queenie slid in across from me. I almost didn't notice her, so focused on not being able to enjoy the food I'd heaped onto my plate.

"Not enjoyin' breakfast?"

"Oh yeah, no. I am. Just got distracted." I then shoveled the remaining bites of food into my mouth, barely taking a breath until my plate was empty.

"Well, you didn't need to rush on my account, but if you're not gonna grab seconds, I can take you back into the kitchen."

"I'm good."

Queenie motioned for me to follow her, and we went through doors that swung both ways. The kitchen was a large industrial space with long metal tables for food preparation and deep metal sinks.

Pots and pans, dishes and silverware were scattered everywhere, and I cringed at the complete lack of organization here. Don't ask me why, but I kinda wanted organizing the hell out of this place to be my first job.

As we moved deeper into the kitchen, I heard two people speaking Spanish.

Queenie turned back toward me and spoke in the most abhorrent Spanish I'd ever heard. "Bienvenidos a la kitchen. Mariana! Hector! I got somethin' for ya."

A tall, muscular man with a mop of wavy black hair and a neatly groomed thick mustache appeared, dusting his flour-coated hands onto his pants.

"Oye! I told you not to speak Spanish, Queenie. It hurts my ears." Hector, I'd guessed, stuck out a hand toward me.

I clasped his dry hand, with a faint layer of flour on it. "Hey, I'm Natalie."

"Hector," he said, smiling so widely I spotted a couple of gold teeth in the back. "Mariana! Ven aquí!"

A woman popped out of nowhere. Like Hector, she had a gigantic toothy smile and wore glasses with thick black frames. Her brown hair was tied back in a low ponytail.

While Hector could have been anywhere in his thirties or forties, Mariana didn't look that old, maybe around my age.

"Hey Queenie, what'd you bring me?"

"Fresh meat." Queenie grinned.

Mariana offered Queenie a playful scowl in return. "You know I don't eat meat."

"Hi." Gesturing to myself, I cut into their playful conversation, as I was eager to do anything to get my mind off of Brandon. "I'm Natalie."

Mariana put her hand out, and unlike Hector's, hers looked to be covered in a sheen of oil. When I shook it, it didn't feel greasy though. Perhaps she just shined.

"Did you get something to eat?" Mariana asked.

"Oh yeah, breakfast was awesome. Thanks you two," I said.

"Pretty good breakfast," Mariana said. "We have some big plans for dinner."

I already liked the kitchen, and honestly, I couldn't wait.

TWENTY-EIGHT

QUEENIE SPENT some time chatting with Mariana and Hector about food supplies and other kitchen related stuff. I kinda just hung back, feeling like a fifth wheel.

"Thanks, Queenie." Mariana nodded at Queenie as she left, and then turned to me. "Let me give you the tour."

Mariana hooked arms with me like I'd known her forever. It'd been a while since I'd met someone this friendly. I think normally I would've balked at such affection, but now more than before, I definitely needed a friend. So I didn't shove Mariana away from me. Instead, relief settled in.

Mariana showed me the stockroom where they had rows and rows of dry and canned food. "We pull water mainly from the falls on the other side of the lake."

"Oh, I didn't see the falls."

"They're really calming and beautiful. Best to visit on a very bright, warm day."

"That sounds super nice. Is the water safe to drink?"

"For sure," Mariana said. "We boil the water before we do anything with it. It's the best way to purify it. Let me show you the barbecue out back, where we do most of the cooking."

"What's for dinner?" I asked.

"Some sort of veggie stir-fry, and I'm making garlic naan. Haven't made it in a while," Mariana said.

"That sounds so good," I said, wishing it was dinner time now.

"You came with that tall guy, right? The one with the tattoos who looks like he hasn't showered in three weeks."

I couldn't help but laugh. That was a pretty accurate description of Brandon if I'd ever heard one.

"Yeah," I said, curbing my laughter. "That's Brandon. He's my . . . um . . . "

Fuck. What *was* I calling Brandon? My boyfriend? Were we back to being fuck buddies again, like we'd been all those years ago? We'd never discussed it. Did people even discuss things like that in times like these?

Mariana must have caught my apprehension in trying to describe whatever the fuck Brandon had become, and she changed the subject. "Can you help Hector and I chop up veggies for the stir fry?"

"Oh yeah, totally." I shot out a short breath,

thankful Mariana didn't say anything further or mention my awkwardness in talking about Brandon.

As I stared at the spread of peppers, zucchini, broccoli, onions, and garlic in front of me, I felt like I'd forgotten how to make friends. When did anyone have time to make friends anymore? I tried not to beat myself up too badly. It was just my first day here. I'm sure my natural charm was in there, somewhere.

I don't know why I felt the need to make friends with Mariana. I didn't want to fuck her like Chloe when I first laid eyes on her. No, this was different. I felt something in my chest yanking me toward her, but I tried to ignore it so she wouldn't think that I was some creeper.

In the evening, Brandon didn't come to dinner, so I ate in the kitchen with Hector and Mariana. I spaced out while they chatted to each other in Spanish. My eyes caught Mariana when she tapped Hector on the shoulder. Her face said, "we're being rude." I honestly didn't care, not feeling too social, my mind swimming with thoughts of Brandon.

"You from here?" Hector asked.

"Oh, yeah. Lame isn't it? Brandon says this place is so *beige*. How about you two?"

"Mexico, but I moved here before all this caca started." Hector gestured vaguely to the air outside the cabin.

"PR," Mariana said.

"PR?" I asked, feeling pretty dumb.

"Puerto Rico," she said

"Oh, yeah, okay, but how did you end up *here*?"

"A lot of it was boredom. I hated my job. It was soul-sucking, and I needed to make the absolute biggest change possible. So I decided to come here, on a whim really. It was a sort of well-planned impulse decision." Mariana gave a half laugh.

Funny, it was the first time I thought about being stuck in a place when The Collapse happened, but it must have displaced a lot of people. "Do you regret it?"

"No way, it was a great experience overall, even if a lot of it sucked."

I had to admire this woman's ability to put a positive spin on even the shittiest of circumstances. I never could've looked at the world the way she did. Maybe that's why I wanted to be her friend so badly.

After dinner, I carried the lantern back to Sunshine. This turned out to be a whole new way of living for me. I still kept my guard, but as soon as they'd closed the gate behind us yesterday, I felt my whole body relax.

Sunshine's interior stood shrouded in darkness until I thrust the lantern ahead of me into it. Fuck, this place looked like the set of a slasher flick. And I totally recognized the irony of that.

I hooked the lantern into its catch and yanked off my jacket and pants before riffling through my pack. I pulled out my book, *Leviathan Wakes*. I'd picked it up at the community library—basically a couple of book-shelves with tons of titles—and started reading it on my break earlier. I flipped to the dog-eared page where I'd left off. Curling in on myself, I read listening to the sounds of the camp: people laughing in the distance, crickets, and finally came the crunch of boots on gravel. Brandon.

"Busy night?" I asked.

"Negative." He dropped his gear on the empty bunk and stripped off his clothes, leaving only his underwear on.

"I mean, I guess that's good."

"Boring. Not really digging it here. Went for a walk by myself after shift." He slid under the heavy blanket and pressed his body up against mine.

"Fuck, you're cold."

"Just move your sweet booty closer," he said.

I felt compelled to wiggle closer to him, and he made tiny little noises of approval. Heat pulsed throughout my entire body, and I didn't feel cold anymore.

"Yeah, you just gave me a hard on."

"Should we do something about it?"

"Meow."

Brandon pushed his body closer to mine, and I breathed out a soft moan, knowing there'd definitely be no resisting now.

TWENTY-NINE

DAWN HAD me into the kitchen before everyone else had woken up, especially Brandon. Of course, I'd picked the job with the worst hours.

Mariana had her hands on a rolling pin making disks out of little dough balls. The smell of freshly brewed coffee wafted into my nostrils, and a wave of sadness slapped me in the face as I thought of Franklin. My eyes went watery.

"Natalie? Earth to Natalie." Hector stood in front of me with a cup of coffee.

I wrinkled my nose. "Oh, no thanks, man. We got tea here by chance?"

"In storage," Mariana called. "The tea kettle is in the back over the fire."

I grabbed a mug and tea bag and headed outside. In addition to the barbeque grill behind the kitchen, someone had arranged large gray stones in a circle to create a small firepit.

Metal racks stood above the blazing fire and on

one rack sat an all-metal tea kettle. The other rack had a long flat griddle on it, like for making pancakes, and thinking about them made my mouth water.

The morning chill bit my face, causing me to flip my hood over my head and zip my hoodie to my neck. I was so tired of the cold. Mariana came out with plates and the flattened dough balls, each one separated by some kind of wax paper, preventing them from sticking together.

She tossed one onto the griddle, and the smell of the fat in the dough solidifying the disks swirled into my nose. I closed my eyes and breathed in the aroma of the tortillas. When I opened my eyes, I saw Mariana twirling, twisting, and flipping them before putting them on an empty plate.

"Those smell so good," I said, ogling the stack.

"Homemade tortillas are great. Unfortunately, I haven't had the chance to eat many," Mariana said.

"Oh, I figured you made these all the time," I said.

"Nah, we don't always have the ingredients to make tortillas."

"Natalie!" Hector's voice broke into my daydream about making burritos.

After I tore myself away from the griddle, tea in hand, I found Hector frantic in the kitchen, trying to do several things at once. I took that as a hint to assist and took the knife from his hands. I continued chopping the onions and peppers he'd started dicing. Freed of that task, Hector went back to cracking eggs into a large metal bowl.

"Put those vegetable scraps in here." Hector

pointed to a large bucket at his feet. "We compost here, so nothing goes to waste. I'll show you the bin later."

I finished the vegetables and followed Hector outside. He and Mariana traded places, and I helped him make the eggs.

"I'll put these out and then make the pico," Mariana said before disappearing back inside.

Holy shit. Breakfast tacos with homemade tortillas *and* pico de gallo. Had I died and gone to heaven? This place seemed too good to be true.

Unable to enjoy thinking about breakfast for long, the sight of Queenie running toward the firepit put me on high alert. She didn't look like the kind of person who moved at that speed unless it was absolutely necessary.

"Hector, I need Natalie. We got zombies coming in through the lake!"

"Sí." Hector nodded to me as if to say "go."

I ran after Queenie. "I didn't even know dead-nots could swim."

"They mostly dog-paddle, or climb over any others who've drowned in the lake. We try to drag the bodies outta there, but sometimes they get so water-logged, it's impossible."

The thought of a dead-not swollen with water made me almost dry heave. They were already nasty enough. I whispered a prayer that I wouldn't ever be on the excavation team, already happily settled in the kitchen surrounded by delicious smells.

A slew of people had curled around the camp

edge of the lake and were firing on the dead-nots. Jumpers. Some of them bounded into the lake like frogs leaping into a pond, and others cleared the water entirely, springing from the shore outside the fence to the shore inside the fence.

I reached for my Bowie knife, ready for some close combat, but Queenie handed me a handgun before I could even unsheathe it. Watching dead-nots drag their legs through the water, leaving trails of blood, like seaweed swaying in the ocean, made my stomach churn.

Raising the handgun, I fired on one I'd been watching slosh through the water. Its foot must've caught on something because it fell forward before the bullet could hit it and plunged into the water. The thing flailed around like someone drowning until it righted itself, using bodies near it to pull itself back up. It whipped its head back and forth, spraying pink bloody water through the air.

It snarled like a feral animal, and I tried to take aim as it thrashed through the water. It must have been a runner because it moved faster than some of the others slogging through the lake.

Fuck, stay still, I thought, trying to fix my weapon on its head.

This one seemed trained on me and didn't want to go down easily as my second shot clipped its ear. When it reached the bank of the river, the speed at which it plowed toward me was unbelievable.

I couldn't get a headshot off in time. The dead-not crashed into me, and I fell to the ground, dropping the gun but still trying to keep its snapping jaws away from me. I couldn't shove the thing off as it wriggled around in my grip, chomping closer and closer.

Not like this. I didn't wanna die like this when there were breakfast tacos in the cafeteria. I wished I was inhaling the scent of those instead of the putrid stink of the dead-not trying to eat me for breakfast. My body ached, and I squeezed my eyes shut. At least I would die thinking about tacos.

The heaviness on my muscles eased, and when I opened my eyes, the dead-not had been ripped off me. Brandon stood over a body that had tipped over, its severed head flung backward. Others campers came running to the lake.

Brandon stuck out one hand. In his other hand, blood dripped from the katana, a new old one he'd found at an antique store that he made me stop at on the way here. I don't know why, but I spaced thinking about the fact that we'd never had time to get his other sword back from Marty. Everything always happened so fast. I snapped to when I felt Brandon's hand on mine, pulling me up.

Fishing through the overgrown grass, I retrieved the handgun and went back to firing on the dead-nots trying to breach the river. The shot I fired when I righted myself ripped through a dead-not's skull, and it fell over sideways into the water.

I jerked my head around at the people crowded around the camp edge of the lake. It looked like the dead-nots had ceased coming, but everyone was still on guard, their faces taut with tension. I dragged my arm across my face and it came back smeared with thick blood. Not mine.

A strong need to submerge myself in the lake to clean off this filth overcame me, and I walked forward toward the water's edge.

Brandon grabbed my arm. "Natalie."

"Please don't," I whispered. "Not right now. Just give me a moment."

He didn't say anything else but answered by releasing his grip on my arm. I walked to the shore, where the lake lapped against a small dirty beach, and set the handgun on the ground. I fished my kitten notebook out of my back pocket and set it next to the weapon.

And I strode into the water.

THIRTY

PEOPLE DISPERSED while I lay floating in the water like a rogue raft. The sun blazed high above me, and it sounded like a normal day at summer camp. People laughing in the distance. Birds chirping in the trees. Frogs singing in the river grasses.

Queenie and a group of campers had dragged most of the fallen dead-nots out of the lake and stacked them up around the left bank, creating a sort of dam of bodies, one they hoped would deter others from trying to breach the lake. She grumbled about constructing a wall there before disappearing into one of the cabins.

I assumed Brandon had returned to his post at the gate. He didn't say anything after I'd asked him to leave me alone, and everyone else must have felt it best to let me be as well. So I floated, eyes closed, listening to the sounds of camp and trying to pretend I didn't hate everything about my life.

"Hey." Mariana's voice broke my lake meditation.

"What's up?" I didn't open my eyes, but I pushed myself toward the water until I washed up on shore like a shipwreck.

When my head hit solid ground, lake sand and dirt burrowed into my hair. I didn't know how long I'd been floating, but my face felt hot.

"I brought you some tacos," Mariana said.

"Oh, thanks." I took the plate and immediately shoved most of one of the tacos in my mouth.

"Do you wanna come in and dry off first?"

"Nope, I'm good," I said, mouth full of food.

"All right, that's fine. What are you thinking about?"

"I'm thinking that this fucking sucks. That everything fucking sucks."

"All right, I agree. I never thought I'd spend my twenties fighting zombies, but here we are." Mariana sat down on the bank next to me.

"You know what sucks the most?"

"What sucks the most?" Mariana asked.

"Fucking Brandon, I mean not like literally. Fucking like the adjective 'fucking.' Anyway, I don't think we're ever gonna be on the same page. Do you know what I mean?" I said, my words coming out in a torrent.

"Yeah, I understand. You know you probably have a lot more important things to worry about right now, and if this guy is adding onto issues in the middle of a zombie apocalypse, I don't think you should be wasting your time or your mental energy on someone who doesn't seem to be giving you what you need."

"I need Brandon." I said that louder than I meant to.

"I'm not gonna tell you how to live your life, but I can see you're not happy."

"I'm happy," I argued, and I didn't know if that was meant to convince her or me.

"I . . . don't see that. I don't know you well, so I can't judge what you're going through. I think there's only so many places where we can find happiness right now, and one of those is from relationships and friendships. And if yours is just making you lay in a lake for hours, I think it's time to reevaluate."

"Thanks for the food. Later." I got to my feet and left her there.

I started walking to who knows where, my head swimming with angry thoughts.

Who did she think she was? She didn't know me.

We'd only met a couple of days ago.

I'd known Brandon for *years*, and I had fought tooth and nail for that man. And my list. He was what I wanted. No, not wanted, *needed*. He made me happy.

Later, when darkness settled over the camp, wrapping everything in shadows, I came back to Sunshine to find Brandon cleaning off his katana. He sat on the upper bunk, his long legs dangling over the sides.

"Rough day?"

I almost hadn't heard him, but I looked up. He didn't meet my gaze.

I shrugged. "I guess. You didn't bother to stick around and find out."

"Not my thing," he mumbled.

"Giving a shit about me isn't your thing?" I spit the words out like they were fire.

"Emotions."

The air that swirled around Sunshine felt dry, cold and caustic, and I couldn't move. Why did we have to keep doing this? This chase where I fell for him and he bolted. And when he bolted, I followed, like a lost puppy. I sat down on the lower bunk, folding the blanket over my legs

I looked up at Brandon. "You're kind of a dick, but I love you. Can't help it."

He didn't look up. "No problem. I know what I am."

"So do I, and I still wanna fuck you, so what does that say about me?"

"We both have scars," he said.

I felt my heart stop, and I couldn't breathe, not expecting him to be so deep at this moment. "I love you, dickhead."

"I have my moments, princess." He took a deep breath. "But I honestly can't say I love you."

Well, that was about right. I had the sudden urge to bury my face in the massive blanket I'd been bunching up into my fists. But I didn't, and I didn't shut up either. Losing Chloe had taught me I needed to tell those I loved that I loved them, no matter the type of love.

"I think love presents itself in different forms," I said.

"Kung fu?"

I gave an exasperated sigh.

"Sorry." What Brandon had his fixed his eyes on now seemed infinitely more important than what I had to say. "Nervous."

That stopped me, and I furrowed my brow. "Why are you nervous?"

I thought he'd been intent on doing anything but paying attention to me on purpose. But he'd been . . . nervous?

"Because it's you." He hopped down, finally looking at me, and I felt his eyes burn into mine.

I swallowed. I didn't have the words, so instead I scrunched up the blanket some more and then smoothed it out. I figured I'd do this until one of us dropped dead here.

Without warning, he crashed into me, almost knocking me off the bed. He enfolded me in his arms, securing me there as if he didn't want to let go.

"You were, are, always will be an important part of my life." I spoke the words into his chest. "Even if you were a dick."

"Still," he said.

I pulled my face out of his shirt that smelled like sweat and cigarettes and looked into his eyes. "I know."

"Simply to kiss you right now would be awesome."

"It would be awesome. Let's do it," I said.

I could see the color rush into his face, and I pressed my lips into his. We devoured each other like this, and it seemed like neither one of us wanted to come up for air.

Maybe he didn't love me in any sort of romantic way. Maybe I didn't love him that way either. Or maybe I did, and it felt safer to deny those feelings or morph them into some other kind of love.

Whatever the case may be, I always became putty in Brandon's hands. I think he must have known this deep down, as he constantly molded me back into someone who worshiped the ground he walked on.

He lay back on the bed and pulled me into him, his hands finding their way along the curve of my body. I wanted to be lost in the moment, but I couldn't help thinking about my list, the one I'd never recreated after losing my unicorn notebook.

1. Survive

2. Get Brandon back

To survive, sometimes we hold on to anything we can. Some hold on to the past. Some hold on to power and control. Some hold on to love. No matter what it is, we grip tight, sometimes until our knuckles bleed, securing ourselves to something that makes sense amid the chaos.

We grip tight, and we never want to let go.

THIRTY-ONE

IN THE MORNING, I awoke with Mariana's words ringing in my ears. Brandon stirred next to me, but he didn't get up. I rolled toward the wall, tracing my finger along the patterns there.

My head was never right around Brandon. My thoughts became muddy. My path became uncertain. Most of all, I didn't know how I was supposed to feel.

I didn't know what to do. I wanted to shove him away. Yet, I also felt a longing, a deep desire to feel him inside me once again and hold on to his skinny body and never let go.

Had Mariana been right though? Had I idealized our relationship too much? Idolizing Brandon to the point where he could do no wrong? What kind of life was one where I'd be waiting around for him to bounce again?

I didn't have the answers to any of these questions, and a sudden urge to punch the wall overcame me. I'd had enough of this, and I crawled over Brandon, eager to be anywhere but imprisoned by my thoughts.

My movement didn't wake him, and he rolled toward the wall, filling the space where I'd once been. I let out a heavy breath, glad we wouldn't be trying to muddle through the muck in my head.

Not like he wanted to discuss it anyway. Talking to Brandon about anything serious required special circumstances. In all the years I'd known him, I still hadn't figured out what those were.

I pulled on sweats and shoved my kitten notebook into the pocket of my hoodie. When I finally ended up in the kitchen, I received a scolding from Hector.

"You're late," he said.

"What? How do I even know what time it is?" I wasn't in the mood, and I'd hoped my tone indicated that.

Hector scowled and pointed to the window with one of the kitchen knives. "Dawn."

"Huh?"

"Breakfast prep starts at dawn. Look where the sun's at. It's well past dawn."

I should have shut up and gotten to work, but today was not the day, so I fought back. "Okay, well, maybe, I'm not an expert at telling time by the fucking sun."

"Hey!" Hector slammed his knife on the cutting board. "If you don't want to work in the kitchen, I can tell Queenie you need a new assignment."

"Hey! Take a step back, you two and calm down. Hector, focus on the meat. Natalie, I need your help with these pancakes." Though I hadn't known Mariana for long, that was the first time I'd ever heard her raise her voice

"Pancakes?" I'd immediately forgotten why I'd been so angry.

"Yes, The Food Crew found some bottles of maple syrup, so I'm making pancakes. Are you two going to keep arguing or are you going to help me?" Mariana placed her hands on her hips.

"I'll help. I didn't wanna argue anyway," I mumbled, even though I was pretty sure I would have continued getting in Hector's face until the end of time or until he backed down, whichever came first.

"Natalie, can you pick some berries for the pancakes?" Mariana pointed to a basket on the far counter.

I grabbed the basket, eyeing Hector with perhaps more anger than necessary as I walked out.

"Pinche gringa." Hector grumbled as I walked out the door.

I ignored the fact that he'd just called me a "fucking white girl" for the sake of harmony in the kitchen. Also, Mariana didn't strike me as the kind to get mad, but her terse tone upon scolding Hector and me sounded like I probably shouldn't be giving her any more trouble today.

When I got to the berry bushes, I saw that they'd exploded with blue, red, and magenta fruit.

What was wrong with me? I'd wanted friends, hadn't I? So why had I stormed away from Mariana when she'd tried to offer me support yesterday? Why had I picked a fight with Hector in the kitchen?

As I filled the basket with berries, using my hand to shade my eyes from the sun, I looked up at the gate. Brandon stood up there looking somehow both relaxed and tense at the same time. Another person perched next to him, but I didn't know the guy. Neither one of them spoke, and I thought maybe Brandon established that atmosphere between them from the beginning.

The mood on the gate changed, and Brandon and the other dude sent some fire over the wall. Dead-nots, I suspected.

Continuing to pluck berries and load up the basket, I let my eyes wander. I still had no idea of how many people actually inhabited this camp. While I wasn't really interested in meeting all of them, Brandon hadn't tried to go around making new friends either.

With no clue how many berries to pick, I just aimed at filling the basket. While doing so, I tried to still the raging storm inside me. Nothing made sense inside my brain. I wanted Brandon. I'd always wanted Brandon. At Summer Camp, the two of us could make it. We could survive the fucking dead-not-dead apocalypse! This should have been my happily ever after, but I couldn't shake the feeling sinking in my stomach that maybe it wasn't.

I liked it here. In this camp with the clean, crisp air, the smells of the kitchen wafting all around me, and everything and everyone so full of life, actual life not dead-not motion.

But I also liked having Brandon curled around me in bed, making me feel like I was the only thing that mattered in the world. No one had ever made me feel that way. Maybe that's why I chased after him endlessly. Could I ever feel this way with anyone else?

What was I missing? Maybe there *was* something else. Something that didn't make me feel like shit all the time.

Dropping the basket with a soft thud, I sat cross-legged on the ground near the garden and pulled out my kitten notebook, determined to make a new to-do list.

Updated To-Do List:

1. Get your shit together.

That was it, the only thing I could write. I underlined it twice to prove to myself I was serious about this.

Getting my shit together meant that I had to start by being nicer to the people I'd chosen to work with. It meant that I had to start by apologizing to Hector.

THIRTY-TWO

WHEN I RETURNED to the kitchen, there was an obvious air of unease. But I bit the proverbial bullet, and with Mariana keeping a wary eye on us, I apologized to Hector.

I decided that tomorrow I'd arrive at the kitchen promptly at dawn to begin my duties. I'd have to work on my body clock, try not to stay up so late reading or doing other things with Brandon. I had to make sure I would no longer bury my head under my pillow when the rooster decided to be annoying in the morning. That animal was the best alarm clock I could hope for.

As usual, I helped by prepping things for breakfast. I carried the bottles of maple syrup out to the long buffet table in the cafeteria. Back inside the kitchen, I rinsed off the berries and started slicing them.

"Do you want me to just throw these in one bowl or, like, separate them?" I asked Mariana.

"Just mix them together." She didn't look up from her giant bowl of pancake batter.

Thinking about fluffy pancakes that melted in my mouth as soon as I took a bite almost made me drool. Having had other Mariana creations, I couldn't wait to taste her pancakes, too.

That thought brought me to butter. "I don't suppose anyone around here churns butter."

Mariana laughed. "I'm afraid not."

"Too bad." I hadn't meant to sound so sad, but I guess, among other things, I missed butter, too.

Mariana went outside to make the pancakes while Hector appeared to be butchering what looked like the remains of a pig. I didn't feel super eager for that part of the training and hoped maybe Hector wanted to continue doing that work on his own.

After I returned from carrying the berries out to the buffet table, I asked Hector what he wanted me to do next.

"You familiar with jicama?" He asked, hacking into a fat pig thigh.

"The vegetable? Yeah," I said.

He pointed to the bowl of jicama on the kitchen counter. "Peel and chop those up with some cucumbers, and come see me when you're done."

I raised an eyebrow at him, wondering why I had to run a salad by him, but I kept my mouth shut until I'd finished chopping everything up.

"How's this?"

"Bring it here," he said.

When I walked the bowl over to him, he pulled a

small bottle with a red, green, and white label out of his apron pocket. Without saying a word, I watched him sprinkle a generous amount of the seasoning on the salad.

The smell of lime and spicy chili peppers found its way into my nose, and I swear my mouth watered. "Fuck, that smells good."

Hector winked at me. "It's my secret ingredient."

I might always be a "pinche gringa" to him, but at least we weren't puffing up our chests in front of each other anymore. I felt more at ease than I had in a long time. I really liked it here.

Peace settled into every corner of the kitchen. Hector went back to slicing the meat, and I took the salad to the cafeteria.

After that, I helped Mariana by carrying steaming plates of the best-smelling pancakes I've ever had the pleasure to serve. Eating them ended up being even better than sticking my nose in them.

Later Hector left with The Food Crew because he said he had a hankering to bring back anything with flavor. He moaned that it seemed like they only brought back salt, flour, and bland seasonings and was determined to find some Mexican flavors to spice up the food.

Mariana and I sat on tall stools in the kitchen over a massive bowl of green beans we'd picked after breakfast. The bean plants had exploded, and Mariana wanted to can them, so they wouldn't go to waste.

A long silence passed before I worked up the

courage to talk to Mariana. Since she'd said those things at the lake, they'd been gnawing at my brain. I worried that maybe Brandon wasn't actually everything I'd made him out to be in my head.

I often pretended to be strong, to be a hardass because this life was hard. It changes a person. Inside, hidden behind my walls, I always became mush around Brandon.

"I guess I should tell you about the kind of person Brandon is. Brandon runs hot and cold. One minute he's snuggling close to me like he never wants to let me go, and the next minute he's run off somewhere leaving me shivering, metaphorically anyway."

"He's like a teenager," Mariana said, snapping the ends off a green bean and tossing them into another bowl.

"I don't think I can deal with my own mental health problems and his, too."

"You are not responsible for his problems. If he can't be responsible for himself, that's not your problem," she said.

"I don't wanna be, you know, but I don't wanna lose him again. We split before. I mean, well, he basically stopped talking to me, just bounced, you know. When we were together before all this shit, we were never really together, like officially. I guess we were just fuck buddies. But I used to be so smitten with him. I brought him cookies, sodas, buttons, and Japanese movies. His loves became my loves: the books, the movies, the music, the TV shows, the comics.

"I honestly feel like I was not a fully formed person until I met Brandon. After, I was the person he made me into. I still carry those traits with me, even after everything that's happened. Even in this fucked up world where none of our old luxuries matter or even exist. For the rest of my life, I'll always be that person shaped by Brandon."

"That can't be true. You're your own person, Natalie."

"I don't know how to define my life without him. I don't even know if I want to," I said.

"I get why you feel that way, but you deserve the chance to find yourself outside of that relationship. You deserve better, a lot better. And there are a lot of great people out there. But I'm not trying emphasize that you just need someone better, which you do. You're an amazing person, Natalie, and it's time you found that out for yourself. And being your own person definitely is more important than finding a nice boy."

"Maybe you're right. But what Brandon showed me, all the cool shit. I dunno. I loved it so much. But I guess, if I think about it, really think about it, I'm the one who made up my mind to like that stuff. I could've just said fuck this." I stopped working and looked at her, my eyes brimming with tears about to spill. "I'm just afraid, you know. Maybe no one will ever understand me like he does."

"We never know what the future will bring," Mariana said.

My voice came out in a whisper. "I don't wanna be hurt again."

"I know. That's scary, and it probably will happen again. Getting hurt is a part of life, unfortunately. But it can get better with people at least. Not so sure about zombies."

"I don't think I'm strong enough for this," I said.

"You're stronger than you think. And I think you deserve to find out who you are without Brandon," Mariana said.

The revelation in her words hit so hard, it almost knocked me off my stool. I never thought I could be someone without Brandon. Who was that person?

"I hope you're right," I mumbled.

She laughed a light, soft laugh with no hint of mockery in it. "I definitely am."

When we finished prepping the beans, Mariana said I could take a break, so I thought I'd head for the falls since I'd never seen them before. Midday had brought warmer air flowing through the camp, and it was a nice change from the cold mornings and evenings we'd had.

Mariana told me to follow the curve of the lake which would eventually lead to the falls. Basically, I'd only seen one small part of the lake, the part where the dead-nots had come over the left bank and where I'd floated.

It was actually much larger than I'd imagined, and I couldn't be sure exactly how long, but the walk took more time than I thought it would. That hadn't mattered though, since they didn't do lunch service, and I just needed to be back to help with dinner.

Queenie had been the one to explain the schedule when she first introduced me to Mariana and Hector. All the campers got two meals a day: breakfast and dinner. Midday, there'd be snacks: apples or something like that.

The Food Crew often brought back stuff like granola bars or crackers, food that didn't need to be prepped or cooked. Throughout the day, people could help themselves to the snacks whenever they got hungry.

By the time I'd been following the lake forever, I'd realized I hadn't brought any drinking water. I'd pocketed a granola bar to take on my hike. I had my Bowie knife as always, but I felt pretty stupid and dehydrated after finding myself without water. No way would I be slurping stagnant dead-not lake water, so I trudged on until I got to the falls.

When I finally got there, the size of the falls overwhelmed me, and I breathed in the crisp air, rich with moisture from the spray. I sat down in a patch of grass before collapsing backward, taking in the sky and the water coming down in a torrent.

I wasted the rest of the day sitting in the spray of the falls, getting up once in a while to steal slurps of water. I sailed my Bowie knife into the surrounding trees, noting that I'd vastly improved since I started throwing this thing. Before I knew it, the sun had crept low into the sky, and I had to get back.

When I finally got to the kitchen, out of breath, it

looked like Mariana and Hector had just returned. Without greeting me, Hector started again on the meat from this morning, cutting chunks of pork from a much larger piece of meat. I didn't ask what part.

"Hey." Mariana pulled two almost comically large pots from a shelf high in the pantry.

"Hi," I said, pouring myself a cup of water from the pitcher designated sterilized water only.

"Hector and I are going to make stew for dinner. His is pork and mine is vegetable. Either way, we need lots of veggies chopped up. Can you help me with that?"

"Of course." I smiled and downed my second cup of water.

"You seem like you're in a good mood," Mariana said as we carried the pots to the back.

"Do I? I mean, maybe. I think I am. I had a nice lunch break."

"Yeah? What happened?"

"I went to the falls. I practiced throwing my knife. Super chill afternoon," I said.

"That's a good way to pass the time." Mariana started removing the core from a head of cabbage.

We sat across from each other diagonally. While she worked on the cabbage, I started slicing zucchini. I thought of fried zucchini smothered in ranch dressing, and my stomach rumbled.

"What food do you miss most of all?" I asked.

Mariana chopped up most of the cabbage and piled it in a bowl. "Ice cream probably."

"Aren't you vegan?" I asked, remembering when

I'd asked her why she never ate any of the eggs she prepared and stayed far away from Hector while he butchered pigs.

"There were so many great vegan ice creams. You wouldn't have been able to tell the difference."

"Why ice cream, though?"

"I feel like a lot of foods I can do without, but every once in a while I just really want some ice cream, and that's not happening these days. Definitely not vegan ice cream either."

"I'd never been a big ice cream fan, but I totally get it. I feel the same way about cheese, only I don't want it every once in a while. I want it all the time."

Mariana laughed. "I get that."

My eyes watered, and I told myself it was because of the onion I'd started chopping and not due to the absence of cheese in the world.

THIRTY-THREE

SOME WEEKS or maybe even a month had passed, and we settled into a comfortable rhythm at the camp. During the day, I'd do my shift in the kitchen, and Brandon did his guard duty at nights. We didn't get to spend much time together other than the hour or so of overlap when he came to bed before I went to work at dawn.

When he wrapped his arms around me, the usual smell crept into my nostrils. Brandon's smell. Almost always cigarettes and sometimes whiskey. Though horrible, it was also comforting. It was home for me.

Queenie made certain that everyone who worked at the camp had one day off a week. We could choose whatever day we wanted. Naturally, Brandon and I chose the same day, so we could hang out together.

While eating breakfast one day, The Food Crew came to talk to Queenie, who'd been checking on people in the cafeteria and making sure everyone was eating.

We overheard them say they'd finally emptied out most of the supermarkets on the main road. But yesterday they'd passed by a turnoff to a small town. Feeling the need to check it out, they found it had one supermarket and a strip of shops with signs advertising things like wine, crystals, tie-dye, and other new age shit.

Aching for a change of scenery, Brandon and I asked if we could tag along when they were getting ready to leave after breakfast.

When we got to that one-horse town, it was so quiet and deserted that I swore I saw a tumbleweed blow by me at some point. A place that radiated peace raised too many red flags, chilling me to the bone

The souvenir shop at the edge of the town turned out to be mostly useless except for a few bags of dried fruit, which the package proclaimed were "Great for hikers!" Pulling them off the racks and putting them in my pack, I doubted hikers would ever be in a souvenir shop buying bags of dried fruit for twenty bucks.

Skipping the crystals and the shops with brightly colored shirts, we made our way to the one supermarket. Two of The Food Crew loaded up their bags with whatever dried and canned foods they came across on the sparse shelves while Brandon and I, with the other Crew dude, opted to check out the storeroom.

When we got to the swinging doors of the storeroom there was an obvious manmade barricade blocking the doors on both sides. Looking through the clear plastic windows on the doors, I could see shelves of boxes, some of which I hoped contained food.

"Hey, help me move this barricade," I said to the guys.

Brandon grabbed my arm. "Nat, wait."

I made a face at him. "What? Why? There's nothing in there."

He didn't answer me. If I had to guess, the word of caution was probably in regards to the purpose of the barricade.

Of course, I knew it hadn't been randomly erected. I wasn't stupid, but I saw no movement inside. All I could see were those boxes. Maybe it had been placed there to keep something out, not something in.

Brandon paced around behind us as we tore down the barricade, an occasional grumble or scoff escaping his lips. He didn't interfere, though, letting us remove all the pieces in front of the door. Once we were able to swing the doors toward us, we ripped down the obstruction inside.

The noise stirred a dead-not, and it ambled toward us like a drunk. There was no big threat here, just this now super dead dead-not, too easy to put down.

"There's nothing in here," I said to Brandon in a real "told you so" kind of voice.

"Yup." His voice landed flat, emotionless.

I hated the duality that permeated every cell in my body when I was around Brandon, the feeling that I needed him, but I sometimes wondered if I could do things on my own without him. Just going into the storeroom made me feel like I could take on the fucking world.

The boxes proved bountiful. Inside were bags of rice, dried beans, and pasta. As we went deeper into the storeroom, we found canned food, too. This only amplified my smugness, and although childish, I stuck my tongue out at Brandon. He tossed it back to me like some weird game of catch.

Carrying this haughty attitude around was what got me into trouble. I thought it would be so in-his-face to open the walk-in freezer to prove that every-thing was fine in this supermarket. When I did so, a flood of dead-nots spilled out, crawling all over each other like an infestation of bugs.

I skittered backward, and Brandon immediately reacted, charging and swinging his katana. Two of the Crew pulled pistols and fired on the front line of dead-nots. Scrambling up, I didn't have time to draw a weapon and instead reached out to grab ahold of a dead-not moving on me.

My arms hurt from trying to hold back the thing gnashing its teeth at me. It sprayed so much blood and saliva I'd sworn it had bitten its tongue clean off. With no desire to check to see if that had actually happened, I threw all my energy into getting this fucker off of me.

Jerking my head to the side, I needed to see how everyone else, mostly how Brandon fared with their dead-nots. Pulling my focus for that brief moment caused the dead-not I had my hands on to push harder toward me, and I slid backward across the tiled floor.

It snarled at me, and I felt compelled to scream back at it. I would've if I'd thought it was worth it. Dead-nots didn't react to sounds the same way people did. Sounds to them meant food, so the louder a sound was, the more likely it would be that it led to someone in danger, an easier meal for them. So screaming at it would only cause it to move harder on me, and I was almost at my limit with this thing.

A runner charged at me, and I used all my strength to move the dead-not in my grasp in front of it. The runner didn't expect the sudden change in position and crashed into my dead-not. When I let go of it, they both went over. The force jolted me back, but I was on my feet before I could take a breath.

No time left to fuck around with my Bowie knife. They'd be up and on me again before I could unsheathe it, so I pulled my handgun and shot the runner in the head before it pounced on me. The other one's leg had bent in an unnatural way when it went down, and it crawled around on the ground while flailing its arms toward me like a drowning man.

I only took a moment to breathe before splattering its brains on the floor in front of me. My lungs burned, and the muscles in my arms ached. I had never wanted to sit down more in my life, but I had to move.

Feeling pretty stupid, sticky with blood, and tingling with the pain of using my muscles more than I'd planned today, I sprung up off the floor and followed Brandon and The Food Crew back to the truck, turning to fire on the flood of dead-nots behind us. Some day off.

As we jogged to the truck, I gave Brandon a look. "Don't even."

"What?" The end of his word flew high like a balloon.

"Your 'I told you so.' Save it."

"'Kay." But he dragged the "y" out.

Brandon infuriated me at the best of times, but I often couldn't decide if I wanted to punch his face or kiss his face. A decision like that should have been much easier.

Get your shit together. How would I ever be able to get my shit together if my default setting was wanting to be naked and sweaty with Brandon? I had the dumbest animal brain sometimes.

Brandon and I climbed into the back of the truck where I reloaded my handgun and fired on the runners that came sprinting out of the supermarket. I barely had time to hold on before The Food Crew driver hit the accelerator hard.

The commotion of squealing tires, snarling dead-nots, and gunshots woke up the entire strip of shops and more dead-nots were tailing the truck before we could get out of the parking lot. Brandon and I were thrown around in the bed of the truck, and I swore I was either gonna be tossed out or I was gonna throw up, whichever came first.

The truck felt like it had rolled onto its two side wheels, but that must have been my motion-sickness-addled brain. I longed to return to that overwhelming sense of peace I'd felt on the ride to this small town when the wind whipped through my hair.

Apparently, The Food Crew thought driving on the road was a pretty bad idea, so they drove straight into an area with stubby short bushes and rocky terrain instead. I couldn't agree with that, as every climb over the earth packed with rock tossed me off my bottom.

The midday sun scorched my brow, and I looked over at Brandon, a little jealous of the baseball cap shading his eyes from the light and heat. The driver slowed the truck, and my stomach finally stopped lurching. I took a breath, and everything settled.

A loud snapping pop came from the tire in front of me, followed by the unmistakable sound of a flat driving over rocks. The truck rolled until it came to a complete stop. I froze, not wanting to jump out of the truck until I'd taken in my surroundings. My eyes traveled over the landscape, but all I could see were brush and rock.

Brandon's hand on my knee shook me out of my daze. "Nat?"

"Yeah, I'm okay," I said, taking a steadying breath.

Jumping out of the truck, we found the driver at the front tire, kicking it and cursing. I couldn't remember his name. Richie or Randy? The other two members of The Food Crew hovered behind him. One, a man with hair down to his ass, and the other, the antithesis, a woman with her hair in short blonde spikes like an anime character.

"Richie, calm down," the blonde woman said.

"Don't tell me to fuckin' calm down, Kris. We're dead, man." Richie balled his fists.

Kris seemed to be the level-headed one here, and her deep voice sounded like it was encased in ice. "We are *not* dead. Let's get our stuff and get out of here. Cody?"

The dude with the long hair nodded and looked at me and Brandon. "You two okay?"

Cody had a high and melodic voice, and I thought maybe I'd been wrong to assume they were a guy.

"Yeah, we're good." I fed my arm into the strap of my backpack.

"Ready to bounce," Brandon mumbled.

Leaving the truck was no big deal to me, but Richie lingered near it longer than necessary. Kris, Cody, Brandon, and I had already started over the rocks.

"Richie!" Kris's voice commanded authority, and Richie snapped his head toward her like a dog obeying its master. "Let's go!"

Richie put his hand on the glass of the driver's side window. I'd never seen someone so attached to a fucking truck. This guy smelled like trouble to me, and to be honest, I didn't care if he climbed into the cab and stayed there.

"Richie! This is the last time!" Kris's voice was low and sharp.

Richie bent to swoop his bag off the ground. He pressed his forehead to the truck and then trotted after Kris.

Silence descended on us as we walked. The only noise was the crunching gravel beneath our feet, shouting our whereabouts. I heard moans in the distance, but hoped the sounds stayed wherever they'd originated from. I'd had my fill of dead-nots today.

I felt a little lost, but Kris seemed to know where she was going. So I didn't question it, hoping she was leading us to the main road. I also wished I'd known how long it had taken us to drive to this town because that would've been something worth focusing on.

Once in a while, Brandon would lean over and nudge me. I wanted to believe this had been on purpose because I'd never felt more exhausted in my entire life. If we weren't walking through a rocky area, I would have collapsed onto the ground.

My alert level faded fast. One place I didn't want to be was in an unknown area, at night, while on the verge of passing out from exhaustion.

I felt grateful for him being here, but I couldn't help but wonder if I'd kicked him to the curb, metaphorically anyway, would I have even ended up on this ill-fated food run?

I don't suppose we had time for what-ifs. Instead, I reached out for his arm and gave it a little squeeze.

THIRTY-FOUR

A ROAD STRETCHED BEFORE US. It didn't look like the main road we'd driven on to get to the supermarket. Before the turnoff for the town, we'd been on a smooth four-lane highway. This paved road, eroded with potholes, was only two lanes surrounded by trees.

What were the odds of finding an abandoned vehicle on this road? As I looked from left to right, I saw nothing. Nothing also meant no dead-nots, so at least there was that.

"Kris, you know where we are?" Richie's grating whisper broke the silence.

"Yes, I know." Kris said in her low, deep voice. "We need to keep moving."

She turned left, and we followed. Brandon and I weren't trackers. Also, we were still newbies at the camp, which meant we were new to this area, too. At least The Food Crew had the benefit of experienced runs in these areas, so we had to trust them.

"So like you two a couple?" Richie asked out of the blue.

"We're, uh . . . "

Sensing my obvious hesitation, Cody broke in. "Kris and I are life partners. We became acquainted before The Collapse. We had plans to be self-sustainable, own our own farm, but this world had other plans for us."

"Yeah, it sucks," I said, trying to commiserate.

"The Food Crew was a second choice for us. We wanted to be in the garden, but that is one of the most popular jobs at the camp and the one requiring the fewest number of people. There was a silver lining, though. In addition to the runs, we also assist the gardeners from time to time, especially when the crops are plentiful."

"I always wanted my own garden." It had been a long time since I had a home or any place to plant a garden, and that cut me to the core.

"It really is a zen experience," Cody said.

"But I wanted a food garden, you know. I'm not into flowers so much," I said.

"Naturally." Cody smiled at me warmly.

Unsure of what to say next, an awkward silence settled on the five of us. It seemed like there'd been obvious tension everywhere we went, and nothing ever really felt like home. Was I wrong about Camp Dewsmile?

As we walked, the sun crept toward the horizon. Light still trickled through the trees and visibility was good on the road. The forest seemed to get denser the farther away it got from the road, but we wouldn't be going in there. It looked like we'd continue on this road.

Cody stopped without warning and then sprinted ahead of us. "Yes!"

"What is it?" Kris's voice was still low, and I doubt Cody heard her with the distance between them.

Returning breathless, Cody said, "It's a car or something, definitely a vehicle."

"Are you sure?" Kris rested her hand on her holstered handgun.

"Undoubtedly," Cody said.

"Do you suppose it has gas? Keys?" Kris asked no one in particular.

"We should check," Cody said. "We have to."

So we approached the car. Before we reached it, Kris held up her hand in a "wait" gesture, and we all froze. She turned her head to us, placing one finger over her lips.

Her steps toward the vehicle were soundless, and I held my breath, hand over my Bowie knife. When Kris got near the rear taillight, she dropped to a knee and peered under the car.

Springing up, she shook her head "no." Each of us took one step forward. Now she stood in front of the rear driver's side window, gazing in.

Kris slowly turned back to us and mouthed the word "body."

Another step forward. Kris moved to open the door, armed of course. We'd known better than to be foolish, living in a world like this for so long.

She put her hand on the handle and pulled. The door sprung open, and that's when the body flew toward her, a jumper, lying in wait for food.

As the dead-not leapt on Kris, the rest of us moved back, drawing our weapons. The force with which it pounced threw Kris backward, and she fired her gun haphazardly before smacking her head on the hard road.

Dazed, Kris didn't even have time to aim as the dead-not ripped into the flesh of her neck.

Cody aimed but didn't fire, tears streaming down their cheeks. Richie froze solid, doing nothing save for dragging his hands through his hair.

Finally, Cody sprayed a shower of bullets into the dead-not's head, almost severing it clean off.

Approaching Kris, we knew it was far too late. She choked, sputtering out blood as she tried to talk and breathe.

The hole in her neck bubbled with blood, and her words were barely audible. "Cody . . . I—"

"No, no, no, mama, I know your mind." Cody said, eyes brimming with fresh tears. "Strain yourself no further."

Kris stretched her arm, spotted with blood, to Cody's face. "Love your . . . mug."

"Love yours," Cody said, stifling sobs.

It seemed like ages or seconds. I had no idea, but Cody cradled Kris's body while gently pushing a knife into her skull, never once breaking eye contact.

Meanwhile, Brandon's eyes darted all around the forest, and mine landed on Richie, who had curled his miserable self into a ball in the middle of the road.

"We're dead," Richie said. "We're dead. We're dead. We're dead. We're dead."

I looked at Brandon and mouthed, "What the fuck do we do?"

Brandon shrugged. We didn't know these people well, but one of them had just died, and another was on the verge of a mental breakdown, if not already there.

Richie rocked back and forth on the ground still muttering, "we're dead." Without speaking, Cody jumped up and moved toward Richie who scrambled up and started running backward.

"Get them away from me!" Richie had moved well beyond hysterical and pointed between the three of us. "Hey! Tall Boy and Tiny Girl, don't let them hurt me!"

"Richie, cease this instant." Cody stopped moving. "I mean you no harm."

Richie took big gulping breaths and clapped his hands on his thighs, panting like a dog on a hot day.

I heard rustling in the trees. The wind. It *had* to be the wind.

And then Richie let out an ear-piercing scream. I looked for what had caused Richie's reaction.

Nothing. Nothing had crawled out of the forest and landed on Richie. I had no idea why he'd started shrieking like a banshee, but he didn't stop, only grew louder.

"Fuck that. I don't want nothing to do with this shit!" Brandon moved toward the car.

Cody attempted to move toward the screaming Richie, who I swore was ripping clumps of hair out of his head. I followed Brandon, but I couldn't help but stare out into the forest.

It hadn't been the wind. One dead-not emerged. Then another. And another. They came faster than Brandon and I could fire on them, and they were heading right toward the shrieking Richie.

Cody turned their attention away from Richie and started firing on dead-nots until they ran out of bullets. Then, they ran straight at the dead-nots with a machete.

Shrugging, Brandon tossed his empty gun aside and went charging in with his katana.

And then there was me. Standing in the road, firing my remaining bullets while begging Richie to stop screaming.

THIRTY- FIVE

RICHIE HAD GONE HOARSE, but hadn't stopped making noise. I wanted to knock him out but I was holding onto hope that he might get it together and be helpful.

"Richie, please!" I said.

Brandon and Cody continued to hack away at the parade of dead-nots. But more and more emerged.

And me? I had one clip left. As I pushed it up into the handgun, Richie took off running.

"What a spectacular idiot," I mumbled.

He ran into the forest opposite where Brandon and Cody were still fighting off dead-nots, so I thought fuck that guy. If he wanted to get himself killed today, so be it.

Some dead-nots got past Brandon and Cody and reached the edge of the road. I turned my attention to them and fired and fired.

Cody's scream jerked my head back in their direction. A dead-not tore through the flesh of their arm, rousing even more dead-nots.

They broke free from the ones feasting on them, pulled a dagger out of their boot, and plunged it into their own neck. Dead-nots swarmed over Cody's body as they fell.

Fifteen feet away. I was fifteen feet away when I ran out of bullets. I was fifteen feet away when the dead-nots overpowered Brandon. I was fifteen feet away when I put my hand on my Bowie knife.

I froze in indecision. As expected, Brandon did not stop fighting, swinging punches when they ripped into his tattooed arms.

"No." Barely a whisper, it was the only word I could choke out.

Brandon looked at me and smiled. I threw my gun, definitely empty of bullets, at a group of approaching dead-nots. Unsheathing my Bowie knife, I took a couple steps toward Brandon.

Because Brandon had been bitten, he was already dead. I knew I'd be next, so at least I could try to take down as many of them as I could before we both died.

My knuckles went white, and as I gripped the knife, I could feel my nails slicing into my flesh. I looked at the Bowie knife in my hand.

I knew what I had to do, and I swallowed hard, unsure if I could do it. He'd taught me well enough, and I'd practiced almost every chance I got.

Throwing it at a dead-not chewing on his bicep

would be pointless. He was surrounded by so many, so there was only one thing left to do.

Mariana's words sounded in my head. "It can get better with people, at least."

I stood like he'd taught me.

I had to close the door on Brandon. It was something that'd been plaguing me for a while, but I could never do it. Now, despite how I had to do, it seemed like the only thing I could do. The dead-nots ripping him to pieces forced me to act fast.

I threw the knife. It cut through the air so smoothly before sticking into his head. I took one last look. His body dropped to the ground, and he was buried under a mountain of dead-nots.

Tears filled my eyes, blurring my vision. I took off running toward the car, as fast as I could. Some runners sprinted after me, but I made it inside, slammed the driver's side door, and locked the doors.

I took a couple shuddering breaths. Dead-nots clawed at the windows, leaving bloody streaks on the glass.

No keys. No keys in the ignition or in the center console. No keys dropped down from the sun visor. I started pawing around on the floor. Nothing. No keys.

More dead-nots surrounded the car. They climbed on top of it, shook the sides, scraped at the windows. They crawled over each other, trying to get to the meal inside.

The sun disappeared, and only a faint light emanated from the horizon. It was dark in the car. I checked the glove box. Breathing heavily, tears wouldn't stop running down my face. No keys.

I patted the floor beneath my feet. I reached under the seat. No keys. I couldn't see through the tears. I didn't want to die like this. Trapped in this prison.

As I reached in between the seat and the center console, something sharp sliced my hand open. And that's when I noticed the rear window was open a crack.

A dead-not shoved its nose into the small opening and sniffed. The smell of fresh blood caused it to attack with more force, and it stuck its fingers through, trying to force the window down.

My fingertips brushed the metal slide of the seat adjuster rack. I moved my bloody hand back, about to extract it when I grazed a piece of metal. I thrust my hand as deep as it could go, wincing as I felt my flesh peel away.

A set of keys, and I let out a low grunt as I pulled my bloody hand out of the narrow spot. Shaking I thrust the key into the ignition. The engine turned over a couple times.

I took a deep breath and tried again. Nothing happened. I slumped over the steering wheel, letting the tears fall in torrents until I could do nothing but scream.

Placing my hand on the keys, I had to try again. I turned the key.

The car started, and I rolled the back window up, severing dead-not fingers in the process.

I hit the accelerator hard. Dead-nots flew from the car, landing everywhere.

In the rearview mirror, I could see their bodies grow smaller and smaller until they finally disappeared.

Full dark swallowed everything, leaving my headlights the only light in the inky blackness surrounding me. My ragged breathing started to steady.

I had no idea where I was. I just drove, the endless road looming before me.

For the first time since this shit had started, I was alone.

No Brandon.

No home.

Nothing.

I brought the car to a screeching halt. I sat there in park just staring into the darkness for who knows how long.

Breathe, Nat. Breathe.

It felt like the hand squeezing my heart had finally let go, and I was free.

When I wrapped my hand around the shifter and thrust it into drive, my head cleared.

It was time to figure out how to get my shit together on my own.

I hadn't been driving long, maybe a few minutes, when my headlights reflected on a sign that said *Camp Dewsmile, 2 mi ahead.*

ACKNOWLEDGMENTS

In 2015, I reconnected with an old friend (one I hadn't spoken to in about 10 years). After our conversation, I started writing this book. I've been a lover of zombie stories for as long as I can remember, and while Natalie and Brandon have always been fully-formed characters in my mind, getting out the rest of this story has been no easy feat. In the future, I don't plan on taking this long to write a story, so at least there's that to look forward to.

As always, writing is no solitary endeavor, so buckle up because there are so many people to thank with this book.

To the real Natalie and Brandon, this story wouldn't exist without you two and your colorful history. Thank you for letting me write your story into a zombie apocalypse.

Nick Renaud, your hard hand as my alpha reader helped me (among so many other things) completely rewrite the ending of this book. I'm super grateful for all your candid comments, and when I say I hope you don't recognize the finished product, I mean that in the best possible way.

Adam Bell, my muse, I am forever indebted to you for listening to me tell you parts of this story time and again. You never got tired of it or me. I love your energy and enthusiasm for my work.

Special thanks to my amazing team of beta readers. Cheyenne Haney, Jessica Abreu, Megan Zalkan, Nicole Trinadad Padilla, Chie de Dios, Gabrielle Brazell, Gabby Williamson, Carly Vair, Ender Chadwick, Oluwa Seyi, and Mike Harney, I could not have done this without you.

I really appreciate Fernanda Perez for coming up with the name Camp Dewsmile. I couldn't have thought of a better name myself.

Carla Peterson, I am so grateful for the sensitivity read you did on this.

Thanks to my editor, Karmen Wells, who gave me tons of insight which was super crucial to making this the best version of the story that exists out there.

I had no idea what this my book cover would look like when Natasha MacKenzie started designing it, but she really hit a home-run with this super cool design.

Thank you to all those people in my life who never stop cheering me on and forever help me live my dream.

And last but certainly not least tremendous thanks to you my dear readers. I continue to write because there are those who keep reading and loving my stories. I wouldn't be here if it weren't for you.

ABOUT THE AUTHOR

Jay Ishino has never experienced any apocalypses herself. She's currently living through a global pandemic though, and that's enough.

Jay is a high school English teacher by trade, a part-time bookstgrammer, and according to some sources, a full-time sarcastic bag of fun.

She lives in the desert with an old sassy French bulldog, a hyperactive chug, and a supermutt. If you ask any of them, a dry climate is best even when it's over 100 degrees outside.

Dead-Not-Dead is a labor of love almost eight years in the making. It's her 3rd book, but definitely the one she worked on the longest. Her other two books *A Year of Rain* and *Blood Like Water* can be purchased wherever books are sold online.

www.ingramcontent.com/pod-product-compliance
Lightning Source LLC
Chambersburg PA
CBHW032354310726
48973CB00007B/2000